Desperate Obsession

ANJI NOLAN

CRIMSON
ROMANCE
F+W Media, Inc.

Published by
Crimson Romance
an imprint of F+W Media, Inc.
10151 Carver Road, Suite 200
Blue Ash, Ohio 45242

www.crimsonromance.com

Dedication

For Dad, who gave me wings,
For Mum, who let me fly,
And for Booj,
Who was always there to pick up the pieces.
xoxoxo

Acknowledgments

Sincere thanks to editor Jessica, Susan Permenter, Sue Carroll and R.T. Anders for your invaluable input. And to Captain Keith Taylor, one of the good fly guys, whose expertise and friendship have been with me for over thirty years.

CHAPTER 1

Jake and a spare chair were under siege at his usual table in the airport coffee shop, and when he saw Alex, striking in her Europa Airways uniform, a head taller than the average woman, he waved. She meandered toward him, and when her leg straddled the pile of baggage surrounding his table, he gave up defense of the chair. "Sit," he ordered, pecking her on both cheeks, "the vultures are circling."

"Nice work, Detective, you demonstrate a real flair for crowd control."

"Not funny, Miss I'll-be-there-at-three-forty-five. What kept you?"

"You can't have been here long."

"Twenty fun-filled minutes, in which time I barely avoided an all-out brawl with the Austrian Sumo wrestler over there." His head inclined toward a large lady in loden green, wearing a Tyrolean hat with a feather.

"Sorry, sweetie," said Alex. "The traffic was horrendous. Then I got to the parking lot and couldn't find my key card."

"I'll never understand how someone so outwardly put together can be so hopelessly absentminded."

"All part of my charm. Now shush, there's more. Terri what's-her-name from Gulf Air—big boobs, Vampira fingernails?"

"Blond with orange streaks?"

"Highlights, you plebe. So you do know her?"

"I know of her."

"She stopped me and asked about you."

"Me?"

"Yes 'me,' you sneaky dog. What've you been up to?"

"Not her, that's for sure, she's a man-eater. You know she and Eddie Barstow were playing more than footsie in a storage locker at the last customs party. Suffice to say he wore turtlenecks for a week, and God knows what his back looked like after tangling with those nails."

"Well, Eddie Barstow couldn't have made much of an impression, because her entire conversation was about you."

"Why the hell would she ask about me? We barely know each other. However, I do know she has a thing for cops . . . do you?"

"Do I what?"

"Have a thing for cops?"

"Oh, I get it, a fishing expedition." Alex patted Jake's hand. "Just one ruggedly handsome boy next door type."

"I'm ruggedly handsome?"

Alex smiled. "Don't get too confident, I still haven't found out if you have any money."

"Typical female." He felt the saucer atop her coffee cup and removed it. "Here, it's still warm."

"Ugh, what is that?"

"Cappuccino the way you like it."

"I like a sprinkle of chocolate, not a crust."

"Pretty vile, huh?" Jake wagged his finger. "You should've been here on time."

Alex's eyes narrowed in her come-hell-or-high-water look as she brought the cup to her mouth.

"Nah-ah, don't do it, Alex." Jake reached for the cup. "Seriously, you do not have to drink that. I just wanted to see if you would."

She chugged the brew and replaced cup against saucer with a triumphant chink. "Impressive, no?"

"See, that's exactly what I mean. I say don't do it, you do; you are without doubt the most contrary female I've ever known. And don't give me 'the face.' A spanking is what you need—a good old-fashioned, over-the-knee thrashing."

"You and whose army, Mr. Big Time Special Branch Detective Inspector?"

"Like you don't think I'll do it. Jeez, if we weren't on duty . . . "

"Yeah, duty, it's a bitch. We spend our life doing our duty."

"Well, I was joking," Jake said, "but even for you, that's cynical. What's up?"

"Nothing, just one of those days."

"No, it's not. I'm your best friend, I know you. We've been doing this coffee klatch thing since our stint at the grief support group and I've never seen you like this." As darkness clouded Alex's eyes, Jake's memory kicked in. Pushing the date button on his watch, September 10 flashed. "Damn it all, Alex, why are you here? Take a couple of days off—nobody will think badly of you."

"The tenth was the last time I spoke to him before the towers came down and he was just *gone*. I wouldn't do it then and I can't do it now. Remember the first time we met; I was so distracted I dinged your car?"

"Of course I do, it brought us together. Uh-oh, don't tell me you hit me in the parking lot."

"Not today, but I was thinking about some things on the way in, the traffic, the crowds, and people rushing all over the world getting nowhere fast." Her eyes glazed over. "Travel used to be enjoyable—you turned up, you flew off. It was fun."

"A lot's happened to change that."

"Amen to that. At least you've been my rock."

"That's me, solid, dependable . . . gray." He flipped the lapels of his suit jacket.

She smiled. "I do prefer you in navy."

"That's tomorrow. You really okay?"

"I am, promise. It's the whole uniform, toe the line, and fly the flag thing. It gets me every time."

"Well, I can't do too much about being a cop for another few years. But your husband left you well provided for; you can quit the airline biz anytime you want. Why don't you get out and see some of the world you're helping everyone else enjoy?"

"Maybe I will. After all, I'm in passenger handling, it's not like I'm indispensable."

"Some of us might challenge that. I'd be pretty bummed if you weren't in my life."

"That's so sweet, now I know why Jessie fell for you." Alex touched Jake's hand. "Why am I being so self-absorbed, you must miss her too?"

"I do, but the last thing she said to me was that she wanted me to move on."

"You can't just forget you had a fiancée."

"It's not about forgetting. It's about finding a new normal. If you don't, the emptiness will drive you mad."

"You're right, as always. And I know in my heart Joe would want the same. Maybe that's why I'm so torn today, I'm a little frightened, but ready to move on."

Jake's heart skipped a beat. This was his opportunity to tell Alex how he truly felt about her. "Do you have anyone in mind?"

She smiled. "I've been thinking that maybe—" A rucksack swiped her from behind. "Yowch!"

"Oops, sorry, ma'am," mumbled a lanky youth through his beard.

Alex scooted her chair closer to the table.

"That's new," said Jake.

"The thinking or the yowch?"

"The 'ma'am.' How's it feel to join the rest of us on the road to decrepitude?"

"I'm thirty-eight, as are you, and I for one am not ready to hang up my dancing shoes." Alex looked around. "But look at this place. It's fast approaching bedlam and survival of the fittest. Tell me one more time why we put ourselves through this every day?"

"We're airport junkies."

"But it's all consuming; we spend our lives here."

"So seriously, quit doing it," Jake said.

"Don't think I can, working fills the void."

"Then at least apply for some vacation time, take a cruise, have an adventure."

"Alone?"

"You won't be alone for long. On second thoughts, I'm not sure the adventure thing would sit entirely well with me."

"Oooh . . . interesting statement . . . little green monster raising its ugly head?"

"Are you saying I'm jealous?"

Alex held up thumb and forefinger. "Little bit."

"Or maybe it's because I know you, your track record isn't good. You attract bleeding hearts like lint. Remember that guy who sent you photocopies of his butt because you said he looked good in jeans? Or the idiot who stuck decals all over your brand new car because you admired his psychedelic bus? What might have happened if I hadn't spoken with both of them?"

"I get the picture: me silly girl, you big, strong protector."

"This is serious, Alex; they could have been nut cases."

"I have a bunch of brothers who could redirect any misplaced infatuation."

"Oh yeah, white bread vanilla businessmen one and all."

"Yikes, that's pretty harsh."

"Maybe. I mean, they're nice guys but I'm seeing lovers not fighters. What could they possibly know about the less-than-gentle art of persuasion?"

"Simon's something of a jock, but on the whole, you're probably right," Alex admitted.

"You know darn well I'm right. I'm always bailing you out of some crazy escapade."

"So how about bailing me out of this afternoon's mess? According to the news, fog was so bad this morning there was no movement in or out for over five hours. This evening could be the mother of all log-jams."

"If you hit overload, call me. I'll use my incredible level of police authority to declare an airport emergency, clear the building, and give you a breather."

"Then who clears that backlog, Sherlock?"

"Right, forgot about a future backlog on top of the current backlog. Emergency, bad idea, guess this time you're on your own."

"Typical male."

"Touché. But look, Alex, all kidding aside, I'm also getting pretty fed up fighting through passengers. We've been doing this coffee shop thing forever, pussy footing around the real thing. We should meet somewhere else—outside work. A bar, restaurant maybe. Would you like to—" *Beep, beep, beep.* Jake hit the message button on his pager. "Jeez, they stopped one of my terrorist watch-list guys in arrivals."

"Terrorist?"

"Yeah, and I didn't tell you that. Look, I have to go. How about we meet—" The beeper squawked again. "Damn, this one's big. Sorry, Alex, gotta go, but we have to talk."

Alex checked her watch. "Good grief, is that the time? I have to get going too, call me later?" She kissed her fingertips, pressed them lightly on his forehead, and wound her way back into the terminal.

Jake watched until he could no longer distinguish her uniform, pressed his own fingers on the spot she touched, and brought them down to brush his lips. *Beep, beep, beep.* "Jeez, yeah right, I got it, I'm on the way."

CHAPTER TWO

Nighttime found Alex at the furthest gate from the terminal, meeting the last flight of the day. Pier's end was reserved for parking aircraft not needed for early morning travelers, and as she stepped outside to get some air, the eerie still and ominous hush of the apron enveloped her.

Pacing back and forth to keep out the cold, Alex realized she'd never experienced so little sound in such a necessarily noisy place, and the surreal harmony of it had her reflecting on her meeting with Jake.

He'd been her best and most uncomplicated friend for the longest time, and understood her better than her late husband ever did. However, his indecisiveness today convinced her he wanted to change the nature of their friendship. She smiled. That might be nice. But what if romance didn't work out, would it ruin what they had? That would most definitely not be nice. Friends with benefits was a notion way too complicated for her tired mind to deal with.

As Alex panned the sky, the myriad stars made it impossible to distinguish airplane lights. And when she looked down to refocus; the tarmac's sparkling ice crystals appeared as dizzying as the heavens. She scuffed her shoe. The ground was still too warm for black ice, which might prevent an aircraft landing. And as she rocked on her toes to stave off the permeating cold, a familiar roar cut through the night. Europa 787 from Malta had arrived. Checking the apron, all ground crews had positioned, and hearing the dispatcher clank up the gangway stairs to the bridge controls, Alex made for the building.

As she tapped in her door security code, something moved beside her. Startled, she turned. Nothing was there. However, upon hauling open the solid metal door, the heat blast from inside caused a loose pile of magazines atop the engineer's box to flap violently. Knowing the potential hazard of a ramp awhirl with unsecured paper goods, she scooped up the pile to dump in the terminal.

*

By the time she reached the lounge, the aircraft was turning onto the stand. Alex pitched the magazines toward the trash bin, but the hasty attitude of her toss resulted in more than half dropping on the floor. And as she gathered up the periodicals, three passports fell to the floor. "Christ," she mumbled, "just what I didn't need." Without a second thought, she consigned her find to the baggage-tag drawer.

*

In the arrivals hall, ninety-three passengers' worth of baggage had spilled onto the carousel. *Funny*, she thought, *baggage handling never fails to hustle for the last flight of the day.* However, when the last passenger had cleared, a suitcase remained. Looking toward immigration, Alex saw they'd held nobody back, so she expected one of the crew had paperwork for a misrouted crew bag or engineering case.

She didn't have to wait long. But, after acknowledging the gold braid and gaggle of pretty girls dragging suitcases behind them, the crew walked directly on to customs. Alex was alone with the circling piece, accepting the karmic gotcha that said no matter how tired you are or what you're in the mood to do, life has other plans. She dragged the large black Samsonite from the carousel and resigned herself to an hour of paperwork.

"Thanks for keeping an eye on it," said an accented voice from behind.

Alex turned to find a route check captain she'd never seen before. Straight from the standard captain's mold—clean-cut, confident, and no-nonsense—he was also drop-dead gorgeous. And an aura of something indescribable washed over her.

"Sorry to keep you waiting," he said, checking the tag, and lifting the Samsonite as if it weighed nothing. "You should have left this on the carousel, it's way too heavy for a lady. Is this the only bag?"

Alex nodded.

"Damn, there should have been two."

"I can check the computer; see if it was short-shipped."

"No sweat; I'll call crew control from the hotel."

She smiled thinly. "Really, it's no trouble."

"It's late, I'm sure there's someone at home waiting for you. Thanks anyway, have a good night."

His hand casually brushed her arm, and a wicked frisson passed through her. She was so thrown off-guard by the familiarity radiating from his innocent gesture; she was compelled to watch him walk away. And aside from the obvious attributes of a man who easily hefts a substantial suitcase across the concourse, he walked as if he knew how to use his body. Alex was so distracted that the abnormality of a captain with his bag in the passenger hold didn't register. She caught herself smiling with an irreverent thought lingering. Now and again, a tiny lust-filled moment made the airport's chaos and hassle totally worthwhile.

CHAPTER THREE

Check-in formalities at crew hotels are usually minimal, geared toward getting tired teams to their rooms as soon as possible; however, tonight crew-control had neglected to book one room. Leaning conspiratorially forward, the captain flashed the receptionist his most devastating smile. "Soozi," he beamed, "may I call you that?"

She smiled.

"It's been a long day, and if I don't get to bed in the next few minutes, I may simply drop at your feet."

"Well, captain, I'm not sure I'm qualified to deal with that," her coy smile hid nothing, "but I do know I'll be in a world of trouble without an authorization."

"So how about I do this?" He handed her a chit from his flight bag. "This authorizes a room, which you can double-check in the morning. If there's a problem, you can take the money out of my hide."

Soozi snapped the chit on a clipboard and grinned—the sort of mischievous acknowledgement that said, *I don't care, it's not my money, and damn, I'd rather do the hide thing.* "Okay, room 304."

*

After ordering supper, and pouring a glass of mediocre wine from the mini-bar, the captain dumped the contents of his wash bag on the bed. He unscrewed the bottom from a can of shaving foam and separated a tight roll of £50 notes from a local phone number. He dialed, but there was no answer. The communication lapse annoyed him, and as he replaced the receiver, there was a knock at the door. He was not entirely surprised to see the receptionist.

"Hello Soozi," he said. "Doing double duty?"

"The kitchen is short of staff, and as I was going on a break, I said I'd run this up to you."

"That's very sweet. Put it on the table."

As the young woman swept by, the captain noticed she had reapplied her perfume and a brushing of color to her lips. As she set down the tray, he moved in close behind her. "What sort of a tip do I give someone who isn't room service?" His whisper caressed her ear.

She turned, smiling confidently. "Anything you feel is appropriate."

"You said you were on a break?"

"One hour."

"Then you have time to help me." He led her to the bathroom. "I really need to relax, and don't know how this shower-head thing works."

Soozi reached up. "Press this white button to select the water pattern." She turned on a spiraling, dancing flow of water. "Turn the blue gizmo clockwise to set the pressure; the higher the number, the more pressure." She reached for his hand, interlocked their fingers, and guided the entanglement beneath the pulsating water. "Feel it?"

"You're right," he whispered, "feels good. Takes me about forty-five minutes for a really good shower—you think it will hold the pressure that long?"

"It will, if you can."

As she turned, he locked his mouth on hers.

From their first exchange, the silent code of paramours had been employed. While the receptionist, pale and blond, contrasted the olive skinned pilot, their minds were colored the same. Nakedness came quickly and, raw and unapologetic, he plunged into her. As foaming rivulets of expensive oil flowed down their bodies, his rhythmic exploration assaulted her senses. In a meaningless coupling that relieved little more than a superficial itch, the captain paid his way, and Soozi blissfully received a considerably larger tip than she'd expected.

*

Opportunistic sex relieved the captain's tension, but as soon as the receptionist returned to her duties, he re-dialed his contact's number. "I want to speak to Jim."

"This is Jim, waddaya want?"

"I want my envelope, you useless piece of shit. I walked every inch of that apron and found nothing."

Jim suddenly sounded more awake. "I left it exactly where you instructed, even went back to make sure you'd picked it up. It was gone, so I split. Look, captain, I dunno what happened, somebody must have taken it."

"You said nobody would be in that area after you. If you're trying to screw me, I will gain a certain amount of satisfaction by beating the crap out of you."

"No need for that, captain, I'll figure it out. Just gimme a little time."

"You're all out. I leave this afternoon, and I want that envelope."

"Wait, I got it. Only two people have codes to the stairs—the dispatcher and the chick from passenger. I saw the dispatcher climb up to the gangway, so it must have been the girl. But why the hell would she be on the apron in the middle of the bloody night?"

"Don't know, don't care, get to the point."

"I'm guessing she saw the magazines and threw 'em away thinking they were trash. I'll go back to the gate, tell the night shift supervisor I lost my ID, and look in the cans. Don't worry, I'll sort it."

"You're the one who should be worried, especially if you don't give me what I paid for."

"I will, captain, I will. Couple of hours, that's all I need."

"And you were supposed to add my flight case to the carousel—where is it?"

"Abu Dhabi." Jim's voice was hesitant.

"What the hell's it doing there?"

"The heat was on; I had to make it disappear for a while."

"You dumb shit, who is supposed to get it back? You know I can't touch the place since the incident with Faisal. For God's sake, couldn't you have sent it to Malta?"

"There was no time. Besides, I couldn't get it across the airport without being spotted. Can't you get one of your flying chicks to pick it up?"

"I could, wise-ass, but I lose a mark every time you screw up. I'm getting pretty pissed off with your fucking mistakes."

"Okay, okay, I get the message, but it's just a bag."

"Yeah, it's just a bag. Sort out the envelope and call me; I'm at the Hilton, room 304."

*

The phone rang at four a.m.

"Captain, it's me . . . Jim."

"At four a.m. who else would it be? You got my envelope?"

"Not exactly, but I checked—neither does security or immigration."

"So if my goods were picked up with the trash, the two grand comes out of your pocket."

"No wait, I have a theory," Jim said.

"You've got five minutes, make it good."

"The trash was all still at the gate; I had to haul it down the pier when a security guard near busted me. But it got me to thinking. The chick who met the flight must have found the passports and stashed 'em somewhere to turn in later."

"Why would she do that?"

"Who knows why a chick does anything, they've all got shit for brains. Anyway, this particular shit-head is Alex Mack. Checked with a buddy in passenger, she's scheduled to work a double shift from seven to seven today, and from noon, she's assigned to cover the arrival information desk. You want me to ask some discrete questions?"

"Not exactly your forte. Leave her to me."

CHAPTER FOUR

The sound of someone coughing startled Alex, and her pen shot across the page leaving a trail of red ink.

"Sorry," the man said, masking amusement, "didn't mean to scare you. I was looking for a friendly face, and you didn't seem too busy. Will you get into trouble for that?"

Surprised to see the captain she'd admired the night before, Alex blushed. "Er, no, I won't. I can do it again. It's not important, er, I'm not busy, er, no, I am not at all, busy, that is."

In the seconds of her babbling, Alex tried to work out why the pilot was having such a devastating effect on her. He was clearly striking in his uniform, although most men look good in uniform. And though she'd heard his voice before, softly accented and disarming, it wasn't that. All pilots have "the voice": a sort of flight-school speak meant to put passengers at ease. The catalyst for her disturbance was his eyes. Intense green and hazel-flecked, they invited her in, making promises not appropriate for anything but very special moments. They spoke volumes and left her feeling something she hadn't in a very long time—overwhelming desire.

"How refreshing," he said. "A woman who blushes. I usually get to talk to a crusty old matron with no soul. Hi, my name is Tayo Vera Cruz."

She self-consciously touched her cheek. "Good afternoon, captain. Can I help you with something?"

"Your name would be nice."

"Yes, sorry. Alexis, Alexis Mack."

His extended hand had a firm take-charge grip, accompanied by a softness and sensuality that did nothing to calm her butterflies.

"My friends call me Alex."

"Well, Alex, I appreciate being invited into the realm of friend, and I know this sounds like a line, but haven't we met before?"

"Sort of." Her skin tingled beneath his thumb. "I cleared your flight last night, watched over your bag."

"Right, that *was* you. It's funny, I asked one of the crew if they knew you, thought we might go for a coffee, but when I turned to point you out, you were gone."

Alex was surprised he'd noticed her, and the knowledge he actually wanted to meet her socially threw her into a minor panic. However, before she had time to sort out her confusion, another Europa agent arrived.

"Break time, Alex, one hour, go."

"Er, I got here late, I've—"

"Perfect timing," Vera Cruz cut in. "Alex and I were just deciding what to do with ourselves."

The agent looked from Vera Cruz to Alex and raised an eyebrow.

"Sarah," said Alex sharply. "Don't go there."

"Me? Nothing. I said nothing." Sarah held up her hands in mock submission.

"So, we'll be in the coffee shop," Vera Cruz winked at her. "Thank you, Sarah."

"Pleasure's all mine, captain, see you two later." Scooping up Alex's handbag with a how-can-you-possibly-say-no look, Sarah pushed her toward the captain.

*

Walking together gave Vera Cruz a chance to assess the object of his attention, and he liked what he saw in the tall, elegant woman with the lean, graceful form of one who exercised. Her hands, long and tapered like those of an artist or musician, displayed no rings. He also noticed a familiar purple striped envelope sticking out of the side pocket of her shoulder bag. "Very perceptive colleague you have there," he said.

Alex looked straight ahead. "How so?"

"She clearly saw the same aura I did."

"Excuse me? Aura?"

"Between you and me. Can't you feel something cosmic happening?"

"Cosmic? I can't imagine what you mean."

*

Arriving at the coffee shop, the pair stood aside for two men leaving. Alex recognized them as Special Branch officers, and nodded at Eddie Barstow, who raised an eyebrow. She defied his silent admonition by flexing into the hand hovering about the small of her back.

The captain steered Alex to a table in a corner of the lounge, pulled out a chair, and placing her back to the room, positioned himself looking out. "Felt some negativity back there. Big guy a friend of yours?"

"Not exactly. Friend of a friend."

"He didn't seem to approve of you being with me."

"Who I chose to be with is none of his, or anyone else's, business."

"As long as he's not a boyfriend. Wouldn't want to step on anyone's toes."

"Everyone's toes are universally safe. No boyfriend."

"Good." He smiled. "I'm not good with confrontation."

*

During their conversation, Vera Cruz put on his best charming, eloquent façade, and with skillful maneuvering, changed the conversation's direction several times in as many minutes. "Why did you disappear in such a hurry last night?"

"Had this double shift today and needed to get home to bed."

"With anyone in particular?"

"I live alone."

"Hard to believe someone as attractive as you doesn't have an admirer or two?"

"Don't judge this book by its cover; I can be a handful."

"Nothing wrong with an independent woman." His instincts had been right about her. "Personally, I like a challenge."

"Not sure what to make of that." Alex fidgeted with her coffee cup. "What about your night? Those flight attendants were probably all over you."

"Occupational hazard, but I do the choosing."

"You're pretty confident."

"You're here, aren't you?"

She grimaced. "Touché, captain."

As they laughed, he moved his hand over hers. "So what's the real reason you rushed off? We could have shared a glass of wine or something."

"Emphasis on the 'something'?"

"Wow, you have a real knack of misinterpreting a guy's delivery."

"Well, you pilots do have a reputation for—oh, shit. Sorry, rats."

"What's the matter?"

"You reminded me, delivery. I have to do something." She unconsciously touched the corner of the envelope protruding from her bag.

"Alex, thank God," Vera Cruz said in mock surprise. "Are they my passports?"

"Er, I'm not sure."

"Did you find them at gate twenty-two? I mislaid them there. They belong to three deportees I'm shipping back to Lisbon today.

Did you see the faces on those guys, are they criminals or what?"

"I didn't look at them, just dropped them in a drawer to give to immigration first thing this morning. But I was late getting in, and then dispatch sent me to the other terminal. And now I'm having coffee with you. Damn it, how am I going to talk my way out of this? I am in so much trouble. Sorry, I have to go and turn them in right now."

As she stood, Vera Cruz held onto her hand. "Alex, sit a minute, let's talk this through."

She sat, shoulder bag clutched in her lap.

"I'm truly sorry if my carelessness has put you in an awkward situation. I wouldn't do that for the world. But we've both broken some pretty hard and fast rules. How about you give me the passports, and save us both a load of trouble. I'm the idiot who misplaced the envelope, so if you hand it back to me, nobody will be any wiser. Nothing more will be said. You won't have to explain why you still have it. And I won't have to sit through an immigration lecture and fill out a mountain of security forms."

"I appreciate your concern, Tayo, and don't mean to be obstructive, but I found this stuff on the ramp. If they're deportee passports, why were they on the engineer's box? You should've been given them directly by immigration or Special Branch."

"So *that's* where I left them. I've been racking my brains about that. I was doing a final walk round on the outbound this morning when Immigration approached me. Before I could get the envelope back to the flight deck, the refueler diverted me to sign for the surcharges. Then I saw an oil trail and went to consult with the engineer. I set the envelope on his box while we checked the leak and completely forgot about it." He reached across and eased her hand from the shoulder bag. "Alex, be an angel. I could get into way more trouble than you. Bend a rule, just this once. I'll make it worth your while." Lifting her hand, he kissed the palm.

*

The spontaneity threw Alex's emotions into overdrive. "I don't know, I—"

"Please, pretty please."

She smiled. Her life had been devoid of tenderness and sexual tension for such a long time, and she wanted to please him. "They are clearly yours, and this is because you asked so nicely." She withdrew her hand, pulled the envelope from her bag, and slid it across the table.

"Thank you." His knuckle swept her cheek. "I won't forget this."

"And me?"

"You too," he said. "You will see me again, won't you?"

"When?"

"I have a couple of routes to inspect, but I'll be back next week. Can we have a drink, go out to dinner, maybe?"

She scribbled her phone number on a card and gave it to him.

He pocketed her number and moved around the table. "I'm really sorry I have to go now. But duty calls." Pulling Alex to her feet, he kissed her on the mouth.

As an unexpected pulse coursed through her body, Alex blushed scarlet.

"Until next week—same time, same place."

"You forgot where you left an envelope; try not to do that to me."

He smiled. "Won't happen, and so you don't get any ideas about making up with the big guy in the doorway, I'll give you something to think about." He delicately kissed her and brushed his fingertips behind her ear and down her goose bump covered neck. "Seems you like that."

"I might."

"Liar." He pecked her on the nose. "Be warned this is just the beginning. Stay safe. I'll see you next week."

After watching the terminal crowd envelop him, it took Alex several seconds to assimilate the delicious familiarity he'd expressed after so short a time. And when she recovered her wits, she was horrified to see she'd been away from arrivals for over an hour. She hustled back to the desk.

Sarah didn't miss her colleague's flushed appearance. "My God," she squeaked, "what have you been doing, you are positively glowing. Who was that hunk? Is he married? Are you seeing him again? What gives?"

Unconsciously lifting her fingers to brush her lips, Alex stared blankly. "I'm not sure."

CHAPTER FIVE

When word filtered to Jake, as gossip invariably does, he wasn't happy. He told himself not to interfere, for though he wished otherwise, Alex was not his girlfriend. And while he'd analyzed the current nature of their relationship and convinced himself his interest was merely concern for a friend, his heart knew the truth.

He was first to the airport coffee shop, and when he saw her, there was no mistaking the fluttering in his chest. This wasn't, however, the time for romance; he needed answers. His customarily warm kiss barely touched her cheek. "Glad you could make it."

"Glad I could make it? I always make it. Maybe a little late sometimes, but I always get here. You don't sound right, what's up?"

"Eddie Barstow tells me you're seeing someone."

"Wow, talk about getting to the point. Where did you drag that pitiful example of tact and diplomacy from?" She clearly expected his usual flippant rebuttal, but he said nothing and his seriousness rankled. "Not that it's anybody's business, but for your information, no, I'm not seeing someone. And since when is Eddie Barstow the arbiter of who does what, with whom? What a gossip monger!"

"Not true; he's simply a very good friend who thought I ought to know."

"Know what?"

"That you were here with someone, in our coffee shop."

"'Our' coffee shop?"

"Don't be sarcastic, you know what I mean."

"Well, he is absolutely correct. I was here with a man, a very nice man. But I don't see what business it is of Eddie Barstow's. And why should you care?"

"You know why I care."

"Do I, Jake? What's going on? Why are you acting so weird? Has this mood got anything to do with the conversation we didn't have time for the other day?"

"Those sentiments look like they're water under the bridge."

"What's with the cliché? I'm not familiar—or entirely comfortable—with this cryptic Jake Fowler."

"From what I heard, your comfort level is currently hovering over the exotic, dark skin, Mediterranean accent, not afraid to show his feelings in public type?"

"What exactly is happening here? Please don't tell me you're having people spy on me?"

"I'm not, but word gets around. You were seen kissing a captain, and you know what they're like."

"Yes, I do know what they're like. And contrary to popular belief, not all women are feeble-minded Barbie dolls, holding their breath for a rich, good-looking fly-boy to come along and sweep them off their feet."

"There you go with the sarcasm again; I clearly hit a nerve. However, to set things straight, I was simply concerned."

"Concerned who I was having coffee with? That's pretty lame. Who I have coffee, or anything else, with is none of your business. I have to tell you, I'm not exactly impressed with this side of you."

"Don't you think you're overreacting? As your friend, I merely wanted to remind you—"

Alex scowled.

"I'm a cop, it's what I do. I'm suspicious of everybody who appears out of nowhere, and skeptical of everything that doesn't make sense. And even some things that do make sense I'm suspicious of, because it's who I am."

"So us being friends gives you some sort of license to have a say in my life? And whoa, back up a bit, why the hell would my being with a captain make no sense? You're presuming an awful lot for someone who doesn't know dip about the man."

"Do you?"

"Do I what?"

"Know dip about the man?"

"Christ, who are you, my father?"

"It's not like that."

"It's exactly like that. Well, thank you Mr. Hot-Shot Detective, I don't need you to cover my back."

"Alex, please, we seem to be off on the wrong foot today, I didn't mean to—"

"Didn't mean to what, spy on me? Enough Jake, I'm officially pissed. I think it's best I leave. Is that all right with you, or do you have to alert men positioned about the building that I'm on the move?"

"That's uncalled for. I care about you."

"This sort of caring I can do without."

"You're being totally unreasonable; I only want what's best for you. You know pilots have reputations for being womanizing Lotharios. He probably has a wife sitting at home, wondering how her dearly beloved is coping without her. He'll just want you in his bed on layovers, and leave you waiting for his phone calls."

"Good one, Jake. Brilliant strategy to win me over. You have officially hit rock bottom. How dare you assume I'll allow that to happen. And how could you even think I'd sleep with someone simply because he wears a fancy uniform and shoves his dick in my face?"

"Yikes, where'd that come from? You're obviously upset, and I'm sorry for that, but this isn't you talking."

"Oh, but it is. I can't believe you have such a low opinion of my morals, particularly as we've shared more of what's in my head than some couples do in a lifetime. You sound like a jealous lover, not my friend, and quite frankly you're pushing that relationship over the line."

"I was trying to help."

"You can stick that sort of help where the sun don't shine."

When Alex left the coffee shop, she didn't see the desolation on Jake's face. He could do little but watch her go because he was at a point where jealousy wasn't the hardest thing for him to deal with. It was switching off the detective. He'd had no chance to explain how he'd tried to suppress his habit of assuming the worst about everyone. Had no opportunity to say the right things and tell her how he felt about her. And now he couldn't shake the feeling that someone he cared deeply about, was going to get hurt.

CHAPTER SIX

While Alex had weathered heated discussions with Jake before, she knew this time was different. They hadn't spoken in several days. At first it was she who refused to take or return his phone calls because it gave her a perverse sense of power. Now, the loss of his company outweighed any damning words echoing in her head. And as she looked around the terminal, it was unusually quiet. It vividly reminded her of the lonely mind-numbing silence after her husband's death. Then, it had been Jake's caring concern that sustained her. Later, when she expressed apprehension about entering another relationship, he'd respected and supported her. He was her rock and her sounding board, and she wasn't sure how she'd deal without his comforting shoulder and his unconditional understanding. It was now clear to her that Jake had wanted to change the nature of their relationship, but timing had been against them. Now the thought that she may have lost her dearest friend cut deep.

Alex sighed. Through cussedness and stupidity she had alienated the one man she knew had the sincerest intentions, and now with another day closing, there was no sign of Vera Cruz, the cause of it all. Vera Cruz—damn him. She had no idea why the pilot affected her so deeply, pushing buttons she didn't know she had. But he'd ignited fires so deep within, she thought she'd self-combust. And though fully aware she was shallow and weak to submit to the innuendo of his words and the promise of his touch, it didn't make her feel any less alive or deliriously out of control.

But that was twelve days ago, and with no sign of, nor word from, Vera Cruz, their end seemed apparent before they'd actually started. Now Alex knew precisely why Jake's accusation irritated her. Because she'd gone out of her way to bury any concerns she might have about the genuineness of her mysterious captain. So here she was reaping disappointment from the seeds she'd so casually sown. She was hurt, confused, and irritated. And silently cursing Jake for being a know-it-all.

*

It was eleven p.m. when Vera Cruz and a first officer appeared outside customs. As Alex watched him, so casual, so unconcerned, something deep inside her welled. She busied herself with a manual as he headed in her direction, and as she listened to his footfalls echoing on the concourse's marble, her skin tingled. He closed in like a predatory animal, primed but not yet dangerous, and when he stopped before her she determined to reclaim the calm she enjoyed before meeting him. "Good evening, Captain Vera Cruz," she said. "Can I do something for you?"

"Depends—how much time do you have?"

"Right now I have no time, but I'm delighted you finally managed to find your way back."

"And I'm delighted you waited for me."

"I wasn't waiting," she snapped, attempting to get whatever situation was between them under her control. "I was closing up the desk; there's a lot of paperwork. Do you need something?"

"I promised the crew a round of drinks, but the bank closed at nine-thirty, and somewhere along the way I misplaced my ATM card."

"Seems you are somewhat of an expert at misplacing important documents."

"It happens. Now, could you reopen that safe and change my escudos for pounds?"

"Sorry, had a lot of payouts today, the float's empty. Might I suggest something else?"

"We all go back to your place and drink your wine?"

She raised an eyebrow. "Flattered as I am by the thought of spending an evening with you and your crew, I have a much better idea. I'll lend you some money and you can pay me when you take the flight out tomorrow." She reached into her purse and pulled out £50. "Will this cover it?"

"That's good." He inclined his head. "I'll repay you as soon as the bank opens?"

"Um . . . yes . . . that's fine." She didn't like the direction the conversation was going.

"Thanks again, you always seem to be helping me out." Pocketing her money, he turned to leave. "Oh, this is a thank you for the passports." He pulled a small silk pouch from his pocket, unceremoniously poured a gold herringbone chain onto the desk, and continued to the terminal's exit.

Stunned by what he left, Alex called after him. "Hey, if you don't pay me back, I know where to find you."

And as the pilot tipped his hat in a mock salute, Alex tried to imagine if any one gesture could do more to make her feel like a complete and utter bitch.

When the doors closed with what sounded like a judgmental whisper, Alex was so focused on swirling the puddle of gold beneath her fingers she didn't see him slip back to the desk.

"Do you like it?" he whispered.

Her raised face flushed. "Tayo, I am so sorry, I don't know what got into me."

"I do. You were punishing me for not calling, and being late."

"I, er, well maybe, sort of."

"More than sort of. I'm a pilot, Alex; I can't always be where you want me to be."

"I know, I'm sorry, it's just—"

"It's okay, you're forgiven." He took the necklace. "Stand up and turn around." Alex felt goose bumps crop up on the back of her neck as he secured the clasp. "The crew changed their minds and went straight to the hotel. I'm not the least bit tired—would you like to have a drink with me?"

Alex fingered the unaccustomed weight about her neck and nodded. And as she came through the hip door, Vera Cruz stood his ground and pinned her against the desk.

"Did I misread you the last time?" He brushed a strand of hair from her face.

"No. No, you didn't, I just didn't want you to think I was a push-over."

"A push-over, what's a push-over?"

"Great, now I have to further embarrass myself by explaining what that is."

"I am eagerly awaiting an education," he said, gesturing for her to continue.

"It's someone who's easily fooled, or maybe a woman who's easy to get into bed."

"Ouch, is that what you think of me?"

"No, I'm sorry, again. God, I'm such an idiot, I think I've been spending too much time alone."

"Then we need to do something about that." With the rest of the world ignored, he brushed his lips on hers. "Friends again?"

"Um."

"I will take that as a 'yes,' and now we'll have that drink. Where are you taking me?"

"Being in uniform, our choices are limited. Fortunately, we can walk to the airline club up the road. It's nothing fancy, but you can get a decent Cabernet Sauvignon, and my undivided attention."

"Couldn't ask for more. But first, button up that coat; I don't want you to freeze to death outside."

"Thank you, that's very thoughtful."

"See, you too have my undivided attention. Now let's go. I'm eager to spend your money on my wine and celebrate me pushing you over."

Vera Cruz's arm encircled Alex on the short walk to The Cockpit, and upon entering the vestibule of the small wooden building housing the airline club, he pushed her against the wall. "It's dark in here. I like it."

Held beneath the hard intensity of his body and emboldened by the insanity of unfulfilled desire, Alex unconsciously ground her pelvis into his.

"Enough, Miss Mack," he said, pulling back. "I promised you a drink." Entering the bar of the aviation buff's watering hole, he stopped. "Holy mother, look at all this memorabilia. How did all this stuff get here?"

Knowing she was going to lose her pilot for a while, Alex addressed the barman. "Two cabs, Nigel, then tell the captain all about your prized possessions. He's a Cockpit virgin."

Vera Cruz cast her a look.

"Inside joke," she said. "It means you've never been here before."

"Okay." He squeezed her hand. "So long as there's no misunderstanding."

The ancient barman poured two glasses of wine and shook hands with Vera Cruz. "Nice to meet you, skipper, you wide body?"

"Ten years."

"At your age, you must be hot stuff?"

"I try." The captain clearly didn't want to talk shop right now. "Tell me about this place."

"That's why I'm here. 'Bout 1945, when I actually flew something other than an armchair, this place was Royal Air Force Baginton crew reporting. Most of the photographs over there," he pointed to a wall of pictures, "were aviators stationed here at one time or another. You'll find yours truly top left, full head of hair, first solo under my belt, grinning like an idiot."

Vera Cruz smiled.

"When the base closed, the runways and hangers were utilized for the first airport here, and when the new rebuilding and expansion came, the place was destined for demolition."

"Until the Flying Tigers roared," said Alex.

"Yes, miss, you're correct. While we lucky ones went about our lives, many of our friends didn't, and we had so many memories, we couldn't let go."

"So you did all this?" asked Vera Cruz.

"Not just me. A bunch of old Tigers and other flyers that jumped to main line commercial petitioned to have the building converted for the use of airline personnel. We told the airport authority we wanted to make it a museum where enthusiasts could keep alive the spirit of the early days of flight. Fortunately the developers liked the idea."

Vera Cruz was already on the move. "Mind if I look around?"

"Be my guest. Guys and gals who'd been stationed here over the years dug through attics, bought stuff at sales, and donated everything. We never stop adding. Any questions, yell. If I can't give you an answer, there's an engineer on the night shift who'll gladly bend your ear."

"Bend my ear, I like that. You English have such colorful phrases."

"And what about you, from where do you hail?"

"No one place. I've been on the move since I was a child. This is a fantastic photograph, who took this?"

"Buddy of mine, gone now. See the B52 over there . . ."

As Alex sipped wine and watched Vera Cruz, it was clear he'd never been anywhere like The Cockpit. She'd felt the same her first time, and it amused her to see a necessarily unflappable captain turn into a giddy airplane-geek as he encountered a gem of information he hadn't known before. It took some time and effort to refocus him back on her. And when she did, they talked almost exclusively about airplanes and working for an airline. Time lost its meaning until Nigel reminded them it was last call.

The couple's departure from the club had none of the fire of their arrival. And after donning coats, Vera Cruz's chaste kiss threw Alex into confusion. Nevertheless, as they headed for her car, one of the few remaining in the lot, she expected him to suggest they share his room at the crew hotel.

"Is this going to be goodnight?" she mumbled, unlocking the car door.

Vera Cruz's knuckles swept across her night-chilled skin. "You're really cold, let me fix that." His hot breath kissed her face. "Still cold?"

"A little . . . here." She touched her mouth.

At first tentative, the increasing pressure of his lips relaxed her, and as his ardor intensified, the taste of his tongue intoxicated her senses. Wanting more than his guarded aggression, she expressed no objection when he unbuttoned her coat. However, the unfulfilling motion of his gloved hand over the most sensitive parts of her body tortured.

"Tayo, come home with me, I can't stand these clothes between us."

"Not tonight, Alex, I have an early flight tomorrow."

"I have an alarm clock."

"Can't do it. I want to spend hours making love to you, not a few rushed minutes before I have to get up and fly off somewhere."

"I don't care. I'll get up with you, bring you back here; just make love to me."

"Next time, I promise; we'll have all the time we need and I'll make it worth the wait."

She pouted, determined to reject any idea of a matter-of-fact end to the evening.

"Why, Miss Mack, I do believe I have annoyed you again. Seems to be a recurring pattern."

"Thought you said I'd get 'dinner or something' this time."

"Ah, a woman who's going to hold me to my word. I know, and

I'm sorry, but we arrived late, it's been a really long day, and—"

Her mouth locked onto his.

"Alex, seriously, stop." He pushed her back. "You're making this really difficult for me. Please get in the car before you push me too far."

"That's the point, I want to push you too far, I want you to go as far as you like. I want you here, now, a couple of hours, a few minutes, I don't care."

"Here in the parking lot?" He laughed. "That's not my style, but next time, I promise, nothing will get in the way."

"How are you getting to the hotel? At least let me drive you there?"

"No need. I'm not staying in town. Crew control booked me up the road."

The airport hotel was a short walk from where they stood, and knowing he could have taken her there earlier, Alex had no words to express her frustration.

*

As she drove away, Alex adjusted the rear view mirror to see Tayo more clearly. And while her heart was unsure whether she should turn around and somehow make her wishes clearer, a nagging head-voice told her to keep going. Motoring into the night, the specter of Vera Cruz quickly faded. However, the image of herself making so obvious an advance toward a perfect stranger, would take considerably longer to dissipate.

She was halfway home before she gathered her thoughts. Why did he blow hot, then cold, and tease her mercilessly? Did he mean to make her feel like she expected too much? And who was expecting what, of whom? Hadn't he made the first wickedly inappropriate move, suggested they get together, and left her craving his company? Now, when she reciprocated, because it didn't fit his schedule, she was again alone with promises.

As she slapped the steering wheel, all she could see was a callous dismissal, and her devastation at his rejection turned to anger. Close to tears, Alex told herself to take a step back. Maybe she was moving too fast. But could a willing woman ever move too fast for an interested man? Might he be playing a vindictive macho game, or was it as Jake suggested? Vera Cruz was married, and simply looking for entertainment. Entertainment played at his speed, by his rules, whenever he had a layover. If that was the case, why wasn't he man enough to admit it? Fess up and let her make the decision whether she has sex with him. She was a grown woman, and with or without Jake's approval, she could choose, or not, to participate.

Alex hated that Jake popped into her head at the precise moment she'd made a monumental fool of herself. And she was mad with him too. What was it about good-looking men? They schmooze into your life, play carte blanche with your emotions, and leave.

With anger and disappointment coloring her attitude, and an ache in the pit of her stomach that only one thing could fill, Alex pushed hard on the accelerator and sped recklessly into the night.

CHAPTER SEVEN

As soon as Alex disappeared from sight, Vera Cruz turned back toward the terminal. He hadn't taken a dozen steps when a British racing green sports car, parked several rows down, turned on its lights. It crawled toward him, came alongside, and he climbed in.

"Jesus, about time," she said. "What the hell was that touching little scene about?"

"Business. Shut up and drive."

An hour and a half into the pitch-black countryside brought the couple to dimly lit wrought iron gates, marking the beginning of a secluded driveway. It was a sharp turn, and after the small sports car juddered across a cattle grid, it sped toward the distant manor house. Set in expansive gardens, surrounded by several hundred acres of farmland, it was Regina Sinclair Holt's family home.

The palpably tense journey ended when the car crunched to a halt under a lantern-lit portico. And as Vera Cruz reached to open his door, the woman's voice sliced through the silence. "Forgive me, I didn't mean to question you." Her hand dropped from the steering wheel to Vera Cruz's knee, and moved up his thigh. His attitude might be cold but she found his body was not. "Will you let me say I'm sorry?" Unbuckling his belt, and releasing his zip, she encountered his growing erection. And as she gently palpated its length, twisting butter-smooth skin against hardened ridges, his eyes closed and his head fell back to the headrest. She squirmed to position herself closer to him, but underestimated his focus. When her face hovered over his, in an attempt to kiss, he grabbed her hair and roughly pushed her toward his crotch.

"You always were a jealous bitch. Give me a proper apology."

The woman engulfed him with her mouth, and gave him the apology he demanded.

CHAPTER EIGHT

When his associate pulled the blackout drapes, Vera Cruz shielded his eyes. "Halfway Pete, what's the time?"

"Five after noon. And you have a visitor waiting. Female, good tits, looks like she has money."

"Local trash removal, she can wait. What else is happening?"

"Calendar confirms the next two deliveries are out of Rome, I set up tickets to Fiumicino. Your contact is a guy called Angelo, owns the Café Anglais on the Via Toscana. He's holding a package that needs to be in Antwerp by Friday. There you'll stay at the Tulip Inn in the Diamond District. Call Gabe, his number is in your hand-held, he'll bring the money."

"The Tulip Inn?"

"Yeah, boss. Be a one-star tourist, enjoy the adventure."

"No really, what gives?"

"This Gabe is a new fence, mixed blood, too young, too cocky—got some iffy notions about his place."

"Do I detect a little of the Boer seeping out, Van der Vort?"

"Might be, but have you looked in a mirror lately? I don't have any problems with you."

"Because I pay well and keep you in poppy seeds."

"There is that. Still, I don't think we can trust this guy's mouth. He doesn't need to know where you usually hold your soirees."

"That's why I keep you around. The Tulip Inn it is. How long has our guest been downstairs?"

"Hit the bell at noon exactly, and brought some major attitude along with the bod."

"Tell her I'll be there in ten."

*

When Vera Cruz entered the drawing room, a woman with pinched shoulders and fists clenched stared from the window. "Mr. Tayo." She did not turn to acknowledge him. "I am not accustomed to being kept waiting." Her haughty voice, tinged with a commonality she couldn't hide, grated across the room. "And had you not been highly recommended, I would have removed myself twenty minutes ago."

When she turned, Vera Cruz noted that, though past her prime, she had once been stunningly good-looking with a dancer's body and legs that ran from her neck down. "My dear, Mrs. Wallis." He took her hand, and brushed her fingers with his lips. "Had I known how exquisitely beautiful you are, I would have dragged myself out of bed at dawn." He'd affected a cultured British accent. "Please forgive me, it will not happen again."

"As you put it so gallantly," she replied, "you are forgiven."

"Tardiness is not a usual mode for me, Mrs. Wallis. However, don't you find that here in the provinces, one is invited to any number of tedious late night gatherings from which there is no early escape?"

"Er, yes," she back-pedaled. "Those occasions can be a problem."

"But here we are at last, with me literally tumbled from my bed, not yet partaken of coffee. Will you share some with me?"

"Thank you, Mr. Tayo, that would be very nice." She sat on one of the room's sofas, and like a parson's wife at a Sunday social, demurely crossed her ankles and straitened her skirt.

"Black or white?" he inquired, holding cream aloft.

"Black, thank you."

He handed her the coffee, and set his cup on a side table.

"May I sit next to you?"

"You're not the least bit like I expected, Mr. Tayo. Yes, you may."

"Now," he added, sitting closer than might have been comfortable under normal circumstances. "Upon your own admission, I am nothing like you expected. So tell me something equally surprising about yourself."

"Must I? I'm not particularly proud of my past."

"Are any of us? We all have skeletons. I was well known for my youthful indiscretions."

"Indiscretions? I think I may have something a little more shocking in my closet."

"It would have to be something truly monumental to shock me, my dear Mrs. Wallis."

"Okay. A lifetime ago, I was Cheri Harris, an exotic dancer in one of my husband's clubs."

"Nothing surprising about that, you have very good legs."

"Thank you. I was something in my day. Anyway, Wallis married me to keep me quiet."

"Go on."

"He made his fortune by pandering to people's basest desires."

"You mean strippers, prostitution, pornography, and so forth."

"Yes."

"So?"

"So now his taste runs to underage kids, and I'm having none of it."

"Go to the authorities."

"And say what?"

"What you just told me."

"And the next day you'll find me floating down the Thames."

Vera Cruz hadn't needed Cheri Wallis's confession. Although she looked every inch the grand lady in the drawing room of his companion's country house, his keen sensibilities had immediately established what she really was.

"Mrs. Wallis, Cheri. May I call you Cheri?"

She inclined her head.

"I sympathize with your dilemma. But what do you think I can do to your husband that a good divorce lawyer cannot?"

"Beat him, starve him, dump him down a well." She spoke without hesitation or demeanor change. "I don't care as long as the filthy pig is dead, and I get everything I'm due."

"Cheri, I'm shocked. What on earth makes you think I could do something like that?"

"Because, despite your evident refinement and purported distaste for confrontation, a very reliable source told me that that is precisely what you do."

"Well, I'm at a loss, my dear, your informant is mistaken. I'm a dealer in antiques, paintings, and object d'art." He could see from the arch of her brow that Mrs. Wallis questioned the statement. "Besides, like me, your husband is a prominent businessman. Wouldn't questions be asked if he simply disappeared?"

He rose to refill his coffee cup and Cheri began to fidget. "Mr. Tayo, I'm in no position to debate the whys and wherefores. I have an eye for, shall we say 'the true mark of a man,' and I don't much care who you're trying to be at this moment. I only know what I see behind your eyes, what I hear beneath the voice delivering the line, and what sort of truth is in back of your walk. You might have fooled me a million Johns ago, but not now. Do we understand each other?"

Vera Cruz ran a finger along an eyebrow and grinned.

"My husband moves in some very dubious circles, and has on several occasions narrowly avoided the wrath of his masters. Let us assume he has once again reached that certain zone of exposure, but this time has overstepped whatever boundaries his partners-in-crime find acceptable. In such a case, could he be the victim of an unfortunate accident, or might a self-inflicted injury follow such a fall from grace? Is that something within the bounds of possibility, Mr. Tayo?"

He raised an eyebrow in tacit understanding.

"Wallis's routines are set in stone. His perversions are an addiction, and he will appear anywhere he is afforded an opportunity to indulge his appetites. The world would owe a debt of gratitude to anyone who wipes his kind of scum from the earth. I know you are the man I'm looking for." She reached down and pulled an envelope from her purse. "We're having one of his ghastly free-for-alls on Halloween night—costumes, masks, the whole charade. Some might even suggest it a most auspicious occasion for the inexplicable to happen. Come early, check out the house, do what you do, and I will pay whatever you ask." Cheri stood to leave, and placed the envelope on a side table. "In the meantime, this is for your time." In passing Vera Cruz, she held out her fingers. She read his eyes and withdrew her hand. "Halloween then."

As soon as Cheri Wallis departed, a panel next to the fireplace opened.

Regina Sinclair-Holt, commonly known as Red, impeccably dressed and coifed, with an air of old money and contempt for aristocratic mores, stepped into the drawing room. "I told you she was ripe, it's amazing what you pick up at the spa. You're going, of course. This could be a gold mine for us." Red moved to the side table, and picked up the envelope, which contained a large number of high denomination bills.

Vera Cruz snatched the envelope and threw it back on the table. "Us? I don't remember there being an us." Then he kissed her hard on the mouth.

A moan echoed in Red's throat. Not of physical pain—to the contrary, the roughness of the kiss fueled more shameful desires. She ground her body into his. "Whatever you say, just tell me what you want."

"I want you to leave alone what is not yours." He pulled her close, ran his tongue tantalizingly over her lips, and removed her blouse. Bra-less nipples rose hard against his massaging palms, and reaching down, he unzipped her skirt. It dropped to the floor leaving her naked. "Unlike you, I only handle what is mine."

Red stepped from the pile of silken fabric, flexed her athletic body, bronzed by some foreign sun, and let Vera Cruz lift her onto a chaise. She smiled as he shrugged out of his clothes and lowered his body next to hers. "Well, whatever you're handling," she said, "it's obviously not enough. I see a little belly developing."

"Oh, really?" His fingers tangled inside her as he nipped her body.

Her squirming indicated she wanted penetration by a more exacting probe. "So I think you need to put some effort into it."

"Not yet," he whispered.

"Now," she demanded, biting hard into his shoulder.

His body responded, brutally hard, calling for her to share his pain. And he powered into her. The harder she bit, the more aggressive his thrust. But he was intent on giving her the full measure of his authority. Dropping his left foot to the floor, he pulled her right leg over his shoulder and sunk deep to his balls. But when her muscles contracted hard and satisfying about him, his was the greater force. Pushing deep to her womb, ignoring her cries from each muscle-jarring thrust, he made her curse his name. And when she did, he drove on, cruel and unrelenting.

Their minds and bodies came together, in power and sweat, through tears and pain. And with orgasms borne from dominance and control, spent bodies were the only "us" that mattered.

CHAPTER NINE

Alex hit the play button and Jake's voice filled the room. She was still mad at him and cut him off. But after pouring a glass of wine and settling in front of the fire, she relented. "Pain in the ass," she mumbled, hitting play.

"Alex, it's me. We can't stay mad at each other. This whole situation is crazy and it's my fault. All of it. You're right, I'm jealous. I'm jealous every time I bail you out of one of your cock-a-mamie relationships. I'm hurt every time you mention liking this or that guy. And I'm desperate every time you're close to me and I don't have the guts to kiss you like I want to. We've known each other so long, shared so much, I thought you knew how I felt. I simply assumed. And that's the crazy part, because I'm a cop and never assume anything.

"Look, I know leaving a message like this is wrong, but I can't be there right now, won't be back for at least a week. It's work; you know how that goes. Anyway—jeez, I hate these frigging machines—I just wanted to say, I want us to be something, something more than we are. Will you consider that? Yes, I know, I know, why the hell are you saying this now, on a machine? Because I have to, before you make a mistake with this pilot character and I've lost you forever. He didn't turn up, right? I don't mention that to be cruel. I just don't want you hurt, because I care so much about you. And I know deep down you care about me. Am I wrong? Am I too late? God, call me, please. I'm under cover so can't talk to you, but I'll hear your voice. Just tell me we can at least go back to where we were. I can't handle kno—"

Weeeeeeeeee. The message machine had cut him off, and as Alex hit the replay button, a tear slid down her cheek.

CHAPTER TEN

Since it had been a dismal day all round, Alex's mind was on exhausted automatic as she trudged to the parking lot. Desperately needing to hear from Vera Cruz, she heard nothing, and confused and needing clarification from Jake, she couldn't reach him.

And as she tried to convince herself that men weren't worth the effort, she remembered how Vera Cruz made her soar. Why did the mere thought of him stir such desire and what had she done to deserve the kind of torture she was now experiencing? Looking up, Alex faced a moon shining piercingly bright. It stopped her in her tracks, seemed to hang impossibly low, and fixed her with its hypnotic presence. It gave her the same strange feeling she'd had on the night she found Vera Cruz's passports. She was lost in its stark beauty when a familiar voice cut through the night.

"You know you have the bluest eyes I've ever seen."

She didn't turn. "It's dark, how can you possibly see my eyes?"

Vera Cruz turned her to face him. "I remember them."

His face was tantalizingly close, and as his breath kissed her chilled skin, the sensuous waves of his presence enveloped her. "What are you doing here?"

"I thought you might like someone to walk you to your car."

"It's fifty yards away; I think I can make it."

He draped his arm over her shoulder. "Looked like you were in a stall here, everything okay?"

"Yeah, just looking at the moon—is it bigger than normal or what?"

"It's a supermoon."

"Sure is."

He laughed. "That's what it's called, because it's closer to the earth."

"So you're an expert on moons?"

"Among other things."

"Like what?" As his body pressed tight against hers, and their lips touched, Alex had her answer.

There hadn't been many men in her life, but no other had made her feel so calm and so in crisis at the same time. No man, not even her husband, had persuaded her into an emotional turmoil where sanity dissolved, and she had to re-evaluate every emotion she'd previously known. She knew her inexplicable lust for him was a sickness, an ague from which there was no cure. He dominated her thoughts, and when they became lovers, she knew her soul would be irretrievably lost.

Her introspection was not lost on him. "You're shivering; are you cold?"

"No."

"So what?"

"You."

"Me?" he asked timidly. "What did I do?"

"You drive me to distraction."

"Is that good or bad?"

"Tayo, this is serious. I'm not a tell-all kind of woman, but I can barely function wondering what you'd feel like inside me."

"Is that an invitation?"

"Seems I remember trying that last time and ended up with egg on my face."

"Not sure what that means, but I'm not flying tomorrow and the airport hotel tells me it's full." He enfolded her tightly, pressing so close she could feel his body hard with expectation.

"How do you keep appearing like this, where do you—"

His lips touched hers with the sensitivity of someone kissing for the first time, and a surprised sigh escaped her lips. Confused, he shrank back.

Alex pulled his face back to hers. "That meant don't stop."

He kissed her hard and deep, but their limited intimacy quickly became inadequate. Vera Cruz broke away from her. "Come to the hotel with me, I need to feel your skin and taste your body."

"Thought you said the hotel was full."

"Stop being technical, let's just go."

Alex wriggled from beneath him. "I have a much better idea." She opened the car's doors. "Get in."

As she started the engine, he laid his hand on hers. "Remember, Alex, I'm not the regular guy you might want me to be."

"Who said I want a regular guy?"

"I won't always be here."

"I know."

"There'll be no going back after this."

She smiled. "Fasten your seat belt, captain."

Nothing was said during the drive home, or as they turned onto her cottage's driveway. It was as if words would break the spell, shatter their concentration, or divert the electricity building in the silence.

A wave of warm air washed over them as she opened the front door, and when she reached to turn on the hall light, he blocked her hand.

"Don't need light." He kicked the door closed. And before the catch engaged, he'd backed her against the wall and locked his mouth on hers.

Anticipation spurred their actions and desperate hands tore away clothes. And when they stood naked, Alex reached down. Her hand barely encircled his penis, but she'd been a long time celibate and her knowledge base was scant. And when he shifted his hips, the heft and hardness of him fired receptors in her body producing aggression that took her by surprise. She wanted no teasing foreplay, no gentle meandering, no encouraging kiss. She simply hitched a leg about his waist, and let him plunge inside.

Gasping at his size, Alex quickly adjusted to their synchronous dance against the wall. His full, deep strokes caused contented sighs deep in her throat, and as his tongue swirled about her nipples, she was transported to another place. In the years she'd been without a man, Alex had all but forgotten how it felt to have such power deep within, and now lost to blind ecstasy, she was unable to do more than surrender to the man thrusting so perfectly between her legs. He seemed tireless, an exquisite machine of muscle and bone, a perfect cure for her ailing spirit, and when he adjusted his stance to massage her sensation-starved clitoris, she exploded with desire.

Convulsing waves rippled through her as she screamed his name. But he continued to drive into her until her legs were weak, and a second wave flowed through her. She hadn't imagined she could come again so quickly and had no idea that any man's action could so completely sap her strength. And his power delighted and frightened her. As a third wave of rolling orgasm wracked her body, it was painful, and she begged him to stop.

He quietly withdrew from her. "Did I hurt you?"

"Yes . . . no . . . it's been a long time." Completely focused on her own pleasure, Alex hadn't noticed whether her lover had climaxed. But laying a hand on his chest, she felt no extraordinary pounding, no change in his breathing, no outward sign of satisfaction. "Who are you and what are you doing to me?"

"How about you lead us to a shower?" he said.

She'd never showered with a man before, and on reflection Alex realized there were quite a few intimacies she'd never shared with her husband. He'd been vanilla; Vera Cruz was triple chocolate raspberry swirl. And now, as she admired the defined lines and bronzed skin of the inhibition-less man before her, she recalled their first meeting, when his walk had given him away.

The shower quickly oriented Alex to Vera Cruz's ability. He remained aroused while the water flooded over them, re-blossomed as her hands soaped him, and corded hard as she led him to the bedroom. Nevertheless, he didn't enter her. He took time to blot water from every part of her, then spread her legs, and let his mouth explore her body.

Alex knew about such things, had seen movies and read books, no matter, she was totally unprepared for the sensations his tongue produced. For the first time in her life, exquisite pain coursed through her, and it was impossible to stifle her screams. Squirming under a torment of his delicate biting, she thought her heart might stop, and as an uncontrollable bliss coursed through her, Vera Cruz drew back and entered her.

Long, slow strokes made it abundantly clear he was no stranger to a woman's body. And moving with tenderness and purposeful aggression, he adjusted his speed and depth to match her breathing. Hovering in entranced half-life, muscles straining to draw in every centimeter of him, Alex couldn't comprehend the way he made her feel. She was at the point of climax when he stopped. He simply readjusted his position, grazed his teeth across her nipples, and resumed his delicious assault. She had no defense but to clamp her pelvic muscles on the tempest raging within her. She attempted to match his speed and rhythm. He was too fast. All she could do was relax and surrender to his total control.

And her submission seemed to spur him on. He drove faster, salt sweat dripping from his body, and when his exacting cadence crested, a volcano exploded inside her.

As she drifted to oblivion, floating several feet above where she lay, Alex never wanted to be without the exquisite pain he inflicted upon her.

*

When Alex woke, vividly recalling what Vera Cruz had done the night before, she reached for him. She was alone.

Rising on her elbow, she glanced around. The room was the same as always, and the house seemed extraordinarily quiet. Was the previous night a dream? Had loneliness driven her crazy, causing her to solidify a figment of her imagination? The nightstand clock indicated 7:45 a.m. November 1, and Alex smiled. How appropriate to have had a major sexual hallucination on the night of Halloween.

The sobering thought of such a desperate act shook her to the core. She needed coffee to clear her mind fog. But as she stood, there was no mistaking what she felt. She was sore, satisfyingly so, and she ached—a good ache, the vigorously worked kind. And when she checked her breasts, there was no doubt someone had used his teeth on her. But where did he go?

In the hall, she passed the place they'd discarded their clothes. She touched the wall where he'd explored her body. There were no scuffs or scratches, no evidence they'd been there. And though her heart felt different, overflowing with love and desire and lust, her gut felt a lonely aching she'd never known before.

In the kitchen, she made coffee, wondering what mania had overtaken her. She could still feel him inside her. Hear steady breathing accompanying his rhythm. And as a twinge of excitement tickled between her legs, Alex knew she desperately needed more. Trying to divert her mind to another place, she poured coffee. But the aromatic stabilizer drew her closer to a realty she wasn't entirely sure she wanted to accept. And as she withdrew a carton of cream from the fridge, she heard a key in the front door. She rushed forward.

"Whoa," Tayo said, clearly surprised to see her brandishing a weapon from the dairy section. "Do you intend to throw that at me?"

She simply smiled.

"Thought you might like something special." He hoisted a bottle of Dom Pérignon. "Are you going to put that down and let me come in?"

Laying down the carton, she walked to him, and as she kissed him, her robe fell open. "Where've you been? I'd all but convinced myself you and I had been a dream."

He playfully pecked her on the nose. "Much as I love being attacked by a naked women in the morning, I, and any neighbors passing, can clearly see a dream this is not."

Alex self-consciously tied her robe, forcing tiny nipple bumps into the silk.

"These are good," he said, touching her.

She blushed and tapped away his hand.

"Don't tell me after what we did last night you're embarrassed?"

"Absurd, isn't it? Where did you get champagne?"

"I noticed an all-night market on the way in last night, borrowed your car, and voila, here it is."

"You noticed a market in the dark? I thought you just had sex on your mind."

"I'm a multi-tasker. Do you have juice?" He poured OJ into glasses, and topped it off. "This really is a waste of good champagne, next time we'll drink it naked." He detected a glint in her eye. "The champagne, not us."

*

They spent the day discussing favorite places they'd visited and Alex confessed that she was a wealthy young woman who hadn't been with a man since her husband died.

Alex learned he did everything first class, loved airplanes, expensive champagne, and Italian sports cars. "You don't give out much personal information, do you?"

"Not much to give."

"I'm sure there is," she said. "I'd like to hear it."

"Maybe next time."

"I'll hold you to that."

55

It was approaching two p.m. when her bubble burst.

"Alex," Tayo said, taking her hand. "You're going to hate me, but I have to go. I'm working the flight to Lisbon and arranged to meet the crew at the airport hotel."

"You said you had no flight today. Can't you call in sick?"

"Can you?"

"If you give me more of last night I will. Please stay, I need you."

"And I need to work. Unlike you, I don't have a ton of money."

"I'll pay you."

He laughed out loud. "Well, that's an offer I have to seriously consider. What do you think a night with me is worth?"

"Everything! Take it, take it all, just make love to me."

"Umm, tempting." The finger he ran down her breast caused an instant reaction. "But thank you, no. What sort of a man would I be if I lived off a woman?"

"A rich one. You do things to a woman's body I've only read about in books. You're amazing."

"I know."

"But not modest."

"Never was."

"Not even a little bit?"

"What's the point? I love women, they seem to like me. I work hard at being good at what I do."

"Aghh! 'They' seem to like me. How many of us are there?"

He counted on his fingers until she looked horrified. "Gotcha!" He pecked her on the nose. "I think you're pretty much all I can handle without putting myself in the hospital."

She cuffed him across the shoulder. "So what would you do if I wasn't around?"

"Knit."

"Now you're teasing me."

"If I wanted to tease you, I can think of a dozen better ways to do it."

"I'm sure you could. But really, what would you do if I wasn't around?"

"Alex, come on, you shouldn't be asking that stuff. At some point you have to simply accept what I say."

"Why?"

"It will keep me coming back."

"Soon?" Her lack of confidence showed.

"I don't know. What do you think about dinner in Paris next week?"

"Sure, and we could have breakfast in Rome."

"If that's what you want."

Alex raised an eyebrow.

"Seriously, this is your captain speaking, trust me."

The invitation proved the right thing to say. Alex moved in and kissed him passionately.

"No more today, miss. I really have to go, there's a crew waiting."

"Can they wait until I throw on some clothes? I'd like to drive you to the airport."

"Be really fast."

*

The drive was a solemn affair, and upon arriving at the crew hotel, tension gripped Alex. "You will be back, won't you?"

"I said I would, why do you think otherwise?"

"We had sex, that's what you wanted."

"You think that's all I want?"

"Isn't it?"

"I can have sex with any women. From you, I need more."

"You're not just saying that?"

"No, I am not just saying that. I'll call you as soon as I arrange the Paris trip."

"You promise, this time you will call."

"Alex, we've been through this. You want me to keep coming back, right?"

"Isn't that what I'm saying?"

"Then you have to trust me." Kissing her tenderly, Vera Cruz left the car. He didn't look back as he disappeared into the hotel.

Alex headed home with the softness of his kiss lingering, and her heart as heavy as stone.

CHAPTER ELEVEN

When Air Porto 397 touched down at Lisbon airport, night was drawing in. Vera Cruz passed through immigration and customs, proceeded to the hotel's desk, and picked up a courtesy phone. He asked for Jovita, and when she came on the line, he asked if there were any messages. She answered in the negative, and he simply said "home."

Pete arrived quickly and after throwing his bags onto the back seat of the BMW, Vera Cruz dropped in beside them and fell asleep.

Sensing their arrival some time later, Vera Cruz was immediately awake, and out of the car. His houseboy took his bags to the master bedroom, and the captain proceeded to his study collecting a pile of messages and several international newspapers on his way.

His study was a singularly masculine retreat, one side of which was dominated by large windows, draped with heavy burgundy brocade. The furniture was an eclectic mix of antiques picked up on Vera Cruz's travels, and to the right of an imposing stone fireplace stood a baroque sideboard. It held an ice bucket containing his favorite Dom Pérignon and a tray of canapés. Throwing his jacket and tie over a chair and the paperwork on the desk, he turned his attention to the champagne. Easing the cork from the volatile mixture, he poured a glass and settled into a large tapestry wing chair.

As Vera Cruz sat back and surveyed his surroundings, he knew the villa was the only place he'd ever call home. Locally, he was just another rich businessman who traveled the world and visited from time to time. No one but Pete knew exactly who, and what, he really was.

With champagne and the feeling of belonging relaxing him, Vera Cruz cursorily flipped through the messages and scanned the newspapers. He was looking for the society pages, obituaries, and stop press items. It was one such piece that caught his attention:

HALLOWEEN PARTY TURNS TRAGIC AT SEATON HALL, LEICESTERSHIRE. A gardener completing his rounds found the body of noted businessman and entrepreneur William Wallis floating in the family pool. Investigators were informed the flamboyant multimillionaire had been drinking heavily prior to, and during, a Halloween party hosted by himself and his wife Cheri. It is believed that sometime between 7 p.m. on October 31, and the early morning hours of November 1, he slipped, hit his head, and had been too intoxicated to help himself from the water. While a routine investigation is ongoing, foul play is not suspected.

A faint smile crossed Vera Cruz's lips as he toasted the air. Pete had once again proven his worth.

CHAPTER TWELVE

Breakfast and messages were out on the balcony when Pete woke Vera Cruz. Looking down on Ericeira and the breathtaking panorama of the Atlantic Ocean never failed to soothe the captain's spirit, and it was this view from the side of the house that came to mind when he thought of home. He had chosen this house because nobody could approach without being seen coming up the hill. But as he looked down, he knew his haven of tranquility was only maintained because he met his business obligations. Now, having enjoyed a few hours of solace, those obligations needed his attention. Putting down the coffee cup, he went into the study and buzzed Pete.

"Yeah, boss?"

"Did you prep the stuff from Red's house?"

"Yeah, marked it 'Halloween Tricks,' and put it with the others."

Vera Cruz smiled at his colleague's sense of humor, and after turning a rosette on the desk's beading, an oblong compartment dropped from the roof of the kneehole. It contained a rack holding a couple of dozen plastic sleeves of microfilm. Isolating the one he wanted, Vera Cruz activated a remote on top of the desk, and a sliding wall panel exposed a state-of-the-art viewscreen and electronics set up. He fed the film into its aperture, and the screen flashed a couple of times, followed by the interview at Red's house. With angles perfect and sound Dolby-clear, Pete's film left no room for misinterpretation, and after a twenty-minute run-through, Vera Cruz reset the film, put on a headset and dialed an international number. The connection was instantaneous, though it took several rings before a timid voice acknowledged he'd connected with the Wallis residence.

Vera Cruz suspected he'd connected with the maid, and asked to speak to Mrs. Wallis. He was told she was unavailable. He made a second, more forceful request, claiming he was Detective Smithson with information regarding Mr. Wallis's death. A short silence was followed by a sleepy but familiar voice.

"Detective Smithson, this is Cheri Wallis, what can I do for you?"

Her acceptance of his familiarity during their first meeting left him in no doubt he could take some liberties. "My dear Cheri, you can do plenty—listen to this." He hit play.

The tape was barely into its stride before she responded. "Who the hell is this?"

"Tayo."

"I hadn't expected to hear from you again. What exactly is it you want?"

"The rest of my fee."

"Fee for what? You did nothing. My husband was high on booze and marijuana, fell in the pool, and drowned. Our meeting was pure coincidence."

Vera Cruz was unused to anyone challenging his actions, especially a woman. "I think not, Cheri. You were wearing a red tarantella dress, your hair was pinned with a diamond encrusted mantilla comb, and you wore a stunning cuff bracelet of diamonds and rubies. Your husband was wearing a navy-blue suit, my guess is Armani, and a burgundy silk tie on which was clipped a single diamond tie tack. I'd say around two carats. Need I go on?"

"You could have picked up that information from any gossip magazine. I'd have known if you were there. Let's face it, Mr. Tayo, you're hard to ignore."

"Well then, Cheri, we have reached an impasse. You owe me seventy-five thousand pounds, and it seems you leave me no choice but to come and get it."

"You wouldn't dare, the police would pick you up before you got halfway up my drive."

"Maybe so, my dear, but then I would have to show them our little cinematic production. I wonder how the authorities would view such a coincidence."

The captain disconnected the call and buzzed Pete. They were returning to England.

CHAPTER THIRTEEN

Sporting generic airline uniforms, Vera Cruz and Pete went straight to Lisbon airport's flight deck ready room, where pilots on standby await their assignments. It wasn't long before the captain struck up a conversation with a SATA Air Acores pilot he'd seen several times. And, as often occurs with such acquaintances, the SATA captain requested and received approval from flight operations to allow Vera Cruz and Pete to hitch a ride as deadhead crew.

SP226P arrived at Manchester airport right on time, and as expected, the flight was ushered to a distant parking stand off the end of the pier. A bus dropped the operating crew, including Vera Cruz and Pete, at immigration and customs. Once through controls, Pete rented a car and they were on their way south.

When they arrived at Alex's cottage, Vera Cruz was pleased to see that though almost midnight, there were lights on downstairs. There was no doubt he enjoyed sex with Alex, and it was important to his operation that he do whatever was necessary to keep her interested in him. For, as with others, he knew at some point, he would actually need her.

The porch's sensor light heralded his arrival and, ringing the doorbell, he was amused to see Alex's puzzled face peer from between the living room curtains.

Her face said everything as she opened the door.

He smiled. "I was passing by and saw your lights. Got a bed for the night?"

*

Pulling him inside, Alex clamped her mouth on his. It was several minutes before they parted. "What are you doing here?" she asked,

"I thought I wouldn't see you until Paris?"

"You know how the flying game goes, things change. Should I leave?"

"I think not." She led him to the living room. "How did you get here? What if I wasn't home? Suppose I had someone with me?"

With a deadpan expression, he fired back. "Co-pilot, took a chance, knew you wouldn't."

"Well, you're darn lucky, because I was about to go to bed."

He pecked her on the nose. "Sounds like a plan, but how about we celebrate the impromptu return of your lord and master? I stopped at a little place I know and picked this up." He pulled champagne from his bag, went to the kitchen, and returned minus jacket and tie, with two glasses full to the brim. "It's good and cold."

Alex took a sip. "Getting to know your way around pretty well, huh?"

"I always know my way around, it's a gift." He put his glass down, sat very close, and ran his hand up her thigh.

"You better not start anything you can't finish."

He gave her the look that haunted her every time she closed her eyes. "Trust me, I'll finish." He kissed her shoulder and ran his tongue up her neck.

"You have to stop that when I'm holding something."

"Why?"

"Because ice cold anything in your lap will cool you down real fast."

"Not possible." He turned her face, pecking her chastely on the mouth. "Let me take this—just in case." With her glass out of the way, he untied her robe and let it fall from her shoulders.

Alex wanted to shrug it to the floor, but he stopped her. Then with tantalizing precision, he ran his fingers around her breasts, up her neck, and down to her belly, and his deliberate avoidance of the places she expected had the silk of her gown tormenting her skin.

Leaning in, she touched her mouth to his, but he didn't return her kiss, and when she dropped her hand to his lap, he blocked her. Anticipation, frustration, and desire cocked her nipples and made her shiver. She involuntarily squirmed under his hand, but she could do nothing about the actions that fired her senses. Like chalk-squeal on a blackboard, a sneeze with no release, a funny bone that is struck, the catalyst for her reactions was out of her control.

He was tantalizing and deliberate as he meandered his fingers up her inner thigh. But when he swirled about her pubis and she parted her legs, the silk of her gown prevented his fingers from entering. With a desperate moan, she unashamedly arched into him. She wanted something of him inside her. And ignoring his earlier rebuff, she undid his belt and zip and took him in hand.

From his hardened length, he wanted her too, but when she manipulated his silken skin, he backed away and pulled her to her feet. He removed his clothes as she shrugged off her peignoir and, holding her close, his penis brushed high and tormenting across her belly. She was led to a dining chair, and pulled onto his lap.

Satisfyingly wet, Alex slipped easily over his shaft, and deeply impaled, she gasped as he settled at her core. She began rocking cautiously high, until she felt his hands circle her butt and lift her forward.

"Relax your muscles, and bear down," he whispered.

And when she did, his depth made her cry out. Her pain came from parturition's secret place, deeply borne and alien. But she was primed well and welcomed every nuance of him. The head of his penis hit hard against her womb, but the ridges of his width dragged velvet-soft inside her. And as they moved, the fluidity of his strokes pushed her beyond the essence of her being. She was transfixed in each second, and transported by his power. And blood pounded in her temples as a delirious distress built in her body. "Oh God," she whispered. "What are you doing to me?"

With breath quickening, something deep inside Alex welled. And when his mouth circled a nipple, and his teeth bit down, her clitoris crested. She couldn't escape the pain and didn't want to relinquish the pleasure. As her orgasm erupted, and her muscles danced in spasm about him, she recoiled impossibly deep. With waves of electricity pulsing through her, she raked at his back and screamed his name.

*

Several minutes saw the involuntary jolts of pleasure subsiding, and she focused on the one who'd brought her to this place. He was smiling. "What are you grinning at?" she said.

"I like to watch you come."

"How do you do it, every time?"

"Told you when we met, I practice."

"Don't want to hear that."

He laughed. "Okay, how about I'll always give you something to remember me."

"Please don't tell me that means you're leaving."

"Would that be a problem?"

"That's one of those 'are you shitting me questions,' right?"

He tapped her on the nose. "I didn't know you were the kind of girl who said 'shitting me.'"

"There's a lot you don't know about me." She kissed his forehead and stood. Wetness spread about her thighs, but it was hers. "Besides, you didn't come."

"Don't have to."

"Isn't that frustrating?"

"Depends."

"On what."

"What you're willing to do for me."

She smiled. "I think that's pretty clear."

Vera Cruz walked to the table, picked up a glass of champagne, swallowed a mouthful, and handed it to Alex. "Take a mouthful, don't swallow it."

She filled her mouth with the frigid bubbles.

"Now take me in your mouth, and don't move."

She swallowed the champagne. "It's freezing, won't it hurt?"

"The effervescence counteracts it, and because I'm super sensitive, the bubbles react on the nerves, and—"

"Whoa, that all sounds a bit clinical."

"Then stop talking and do it."

Alex took more champagne, and him, into her mouth. He moved slowly as he held the back of her head. She could see his face relax, and though he was close to climax, she didn't move. Then as his speed increased and the bubbles in her mouth expanded tenfold, he erupted in her mouth. His life force pulsed in a salt-sweet bubbling explosion. And it was like no champagne cocktail she'd ever tasted.

*

When Alex woke at ten-thirty, an ache resonating in her belly and thighs, she experienced a warmth and contentment she'd not felt in years. Hearing Vera Cruz moving about in the kitchen, she dragged herself out of bed, toed into her slippers, and draped her peignoir about her.

As she entered the kitchen, he laughed at her state of disrepair. "Morning. You look like you went ten rounds with Mohammed Ali."

"Went ten rounds with somebody."

"You need to get more exercise."

She planted a deliberately sloppy kiss on his forehead and poured coffee. "Quiet, mister. I can keep pace with Ali any time.

You? That's a whole other story. Let me have some coffee and I'll be ready for a rematch."

"No can do, baby, was on stand-by and got called out. I'm away to Malta. Number one is picking me up soon."

"Will you be back tonight?"

"No. I'm running down to Tripoli tomorrow."

"Will I ever have you for more than one night?"

"The state you're in, I'm not sure you could handle me for more than one night."

"Try me."

"Maybe I will. Come here." She sat on his lap as he kissed her hard and deep. His hand moved inside her robe, finding rigid nipples. "Okay, so it's clear you want me, but what if I don't want you?"

"You lie." As she left his lap, her hand brushed his crotch. "You lie big-time. I'm taking a shower, come join me?"

He smiled and continued to sip his coffee.

*

When Alex went downstairs after her shower, Vera Cruz was gone. Looking around she saw absolutely no evidence he'd ever been there. The kitchen was spotless, chairs were neat around the table and even the coffee pot and cups were washed and put away. She couldn't help wondering what strange manner of man she was falling in love with.

CHAPTER FOURTEEN

When Pete pulled up to the cottage gate, Vera Cruz was waiting. As the captain settled into the Range Rover, and helped himself to the orange juice in the cup holder, Pete headed up country to Red's house. By two p.m., they were out of uniform, on their way to Cheri Wallis's house.

*

Vera Cruz handed the servant a police identity card in the name of Inspector Blackwell. And after it was presented, the captain was ushered into the drawing room.

The new owner of the hall was staring out the window. "Are you going to make a habit of impersonating police officers?"

"Until you let me in under my own steam, I guess I'll have to."

Cheri Wallis turned and gave a coquettish smile. "Mr. Tayo, seriously . . . " When his demeanor remained unchanged, she seemed to realize it was neither the time nor place for such a ploy. "I'm not sure I'm about to let that happen. Now, to what do I owe this pleasure?"

"As I told you on the phone, I came to finalize our arrangement."

"Ah, yes. The arrangement." She began pacing to avoid looking in his eyes. "Assuming I agree to your demands, I'm not a fool. What assurance do I have that I won't be paying your particular brand of piper for the rest of my life?"

"Cheri, I'm shocked. You think me a common blackmailer?"

"I say again, what assurance do I have?"

"My word."

She let out a hollow laugh. "The word of a murderer doesn't exactly inspire confidence. I want the film."

Reaching into his pocket, Vera Cruz pulled out a small plastic sleeve. "Of course; I will be happy to give you what you pay for." He threw the microfilm onto a sofa table in front of her.

"What's that?"

"Microfilm."

"And where are the CDs, DVDs, flash drives, power sticks . . . whatever you people call the modern devices."

"*We people* don't use those mediums because the authorities expect them and have ways of detecting them."

"So there are no copies?"

"No copies."

"What if I throw it in the fire right now, call the police, and say you broke in trying to rob me. It would be your word against mine."

He fixed her with hypnotic eyes. "We both know if you do that, I will have to say my piece and that will undoubtedly open you to unwelcome scrutiny."

"I can handle it; I'm a well-respected member of this community."

"Maybe, but given the right lead, it wouldn't be difficult for anyone to find out what you used to be. Or how your newfound respectability might be a big fat reason for wanting your not-so-upright husband dead. Things could get very uncomfortable, and you'd most certainly lose all this." Vera Cruz made an expansive gesture with his hand. "May I have a drink?" He poured himself a brandy and inclined an empty glass toward her. "Can I get you one?"

"You really are a smooth customer." She rolled the microfilm nervously between her fingers. "I could simply have you thrown out."

"But you won't."

"No, I won't." She threw the film into the fire, and watched as it sizzled and disappeared. "I'll have the same as you."

Vera Cruz poured the brandy and delivered it, making sure as she took the glass, his fingers brushed hers. She didn't pull away. Vera Cruz smiled, and joined her on the sofa. "You're a very attractive woman, Cheri. I can't imagine why your husband preferred young women."

"Because they're nymphomaniacs and hungry opportunists willing to give him any perverted thing he wants."

"And you are not?"

The cutting remark hit her squarely between the eyes, but the momentary silence was replaced by a charmingly infectious giggle. "Well, two out of three ain't bad."

"So, my dear, now we've cleared the air, what are we to do?"

She dragged her fingers up his thigh. "I'll give you your money, of course. Wait here."

The Wallis's study was left of the drawing room through an imposing Tudor style doorway. Vera Cruz watched intently knowing Pete was somewhere inside, but as Cheri closed the door, all he caught was a glimpse of inlaid paneling and tracery bookcases. He had a distinct liking for buildings of grandeur and it was evident from the opulence of the furniture, paintings, and object d'art, that William Wallis had spent a considerable amount of money over the years. Now it all belonged to Cheri. Given time, and not a lot of effort on his part, he knew he'd be welcome in this desperately lonely woman's life. But he couldn't help wondering— did this easily pickable woman have one too many issues?

*

Vera Cruz saw Cheri's reflection approaching, and turned as she held out a blue moneybag. However, when his fingers brushed hers, a small electric shock passed between them. Sharply withdrawn hands had the bag dropping to the floor. And when they both bent to retrieve it, their heads tapped. It brought a smile from both, and Vera Cruz reached out to caress Cheri's hurt spot.

"You okay?"

"Yes, thank you, it's nothing." She sounded like she hadn't known such gentleness in a very long time. "Mr. Tayo, you surprise me again; you're very gallant for a man in your profession."

"And what profession is that, my dear?" Vera Cruz took her hand and kissed the palm. And when she neither pulled away nor protested; his lips brushed the place their heads had touched.

"You'd better leave before this gets out of hand." Her throaty voice betrayed her true feelings.

"Do you really want me to?"

"No, but do it anyway. A liaison with a man like you wouldn't go unnoticed. I'm still under investigation, you know."

Vera Cruz did know, but wasn't worried by it. In the early years, he'd been in a dozen similar situations in which lonely, aging women craving his brand of love and affection paid significant amounts of money to have him make them feel good. He wasn't caught then, and knew enough not to be detected now. And though he momentarily regretted being denied the opportunity to boost his profits, he understood her reticence. "As you wish." He brushed her outstretched hand with his lips, wedged the moneybag under his arm, and headed toward the door.

"Aren't you going to count it?"

He turned and smiled warmly. "I trust you. Besides, if it's not right, I'll be back."

*

The car pulled away as soon as Vera Cruz climbed in. "So, did you have enough time to find anything useful?"

"Ordinarily, no," said Pete. "But it really helps when you have a dumb bitch who mumbles the combination as she's opening the thing. Anyway, there was a shit-load of easily convertible paper goods. I took a few, but if you want me to go back and get them all, it's no sweat. And look at these." Pete pulled two velvet pouches from the door pocket and dropped them on the moneybag in Vera Cruz's lap.

Loosening the rope on the smallest pouch, the captain upended it into his hand. "What do you think; a hundred stones?"

"Sounds right. Tried to pick 'em between two and four carats."

"Except these." Vera Cruz separated half a dozen considerably larger, and one in particular. "This one must be ten carats."

"Thought you'd like that."

"Was this the only one?"

"You kidding? That old bastard Wallis stashed a fortune in there. The old lady probably won't even notice these are gone. Open the large pouch."

"Krugerrand . . . nice . . . and what's this . . . platinum?"

"The vault was filthy with bullion. And check out the jewelry—Archie can easily re-set that lot."

"This is good stuff, Pete. You can have all the gem set pieces except this one." The captain pulled out a large heart-shaped diamond pendant. "It's too unusual to risk selling, and only the center stone is big enough to re-cut."

"You have something else in mind for it?"

"Peace offering."

Pete smiled. "Last tango in Paris is out then."

"You know me so well."

*

Deep country darkness surrounded as they pulled up at Alex's cottage. Vera Cruz knew she was at work, and pulling an envelope from his bag, he scribbled, *Sorry about Paris, I'll call you later* on it. Then he dropped in the pendant and pushed the envelope through the letterbox.

CHAPTER FIFTEEN

Alex entered the kitchen to find her message light blinking. She'd torn open the envelope as soon as she'd found it on the hall carpet, and was sure Vera Cruz was calling to ask if she liked the pendant. However, upon hitting the play button, Jake's voice echoed.

"Alex, what can I say? I should have found a way to call you sooner. I don't deserve you, I'm an idiot, an ingrate, a clod. I am so sorry. Could we meet for coffee, but not the airport? I know that under the circumstances—my selfish ego, not yours—it's asking a lot. But will you meet me at Java Julia in the High Street at eleven a.m. tomorrow? I'll wait half an hour. Please be there."

*

Alex walked in looking as serene and unattainable as Jake had ever seen her. His heart skipped nervously as she approached, but when she smiled warmly, he knew they were still best friends. Meeting Alex away from the airport had been important for what he had to say. But now he faced her, his nemesis butterflies returned. He'd told himself a dozen times that he was a cop, and words shouldn't intimidate. But no amount of encouragement from any of his still small voices had thus far convinced him it would be easy to tell her how he truly felt.

*

When Alex reached the table, Jake kissed her on both cheeks, and held her in his embrace. "I'm jealous, I admit it. Do you forgive me?"

75

"There's nothing to forgive. You're my best friend and you worry about me." Alex had never felt such warmth from his kiss, and when he released her from the hug, his strong capable hand, so gentle on her shoulder, ran down her arm to linger at her fingertips. "Everything is okay, really." It was the first time he'd ever caressed her in so intimate a way, and she'd had no idea his touch could arouse sexual feelings in her. She was stunned that after all the years they'd known each other, his first gesture beyond friendship had made her feel so extraordinarily needed. "So, talk to me. What have you been up to?"

Jake produced a posy of wild flowers and handed them to her. "I was told to stop and smell the roses. I know you're not particularly fond of them, so I chose these."

Alex realized she was looking at a different man than the platonic friend she'd known before. "They're beautiful, thank you. Now, you didn't call me here to give me flowers—what's happening in that head of yours?"

"I was afraid I'd lost you. I made accusations and assumed too much. Being a cop is not always easy, and it's especially hard on the ones we love."

She'd always seen Jake as wholesome, steadfast, and reliable, the complete opposite of the dashing, spontaneous, potentially dangerous Vera Cruz. And while she had no idea why her lover should cross her mind at the precise moment Jake chose to open himself to her, she was now very aware that they each in their own way could pull emotions from her she'd spent years repressing. The vulnerable consideration Jake showed her was adorable, and Alex knew as she looked into his eyes that his were the purest of intentions. Such a contrast to the danger in Vera Cruz's. She blushed remembering some of the things he had done to her body. But the captain was for another time. She needed to focus on the man sitting opposite.

"Jake, let's get one thing clear. You will always be my rock. The guy I turn to when I'm in trouble, and God knows I've had my share of that. Nothing will ever change the way I feel about you."

"So I don't have to relegate my opinions to where the sun don't shine?"

"Did I really tell you to do that?"

He smiled, pulled out his notebook, and consulted a page. "Yes, ma'am, you most certainly did."

"Then I'm the one who needs to say sorry. I was over sensitive. I should be grateful you're looking out for me."

"So now we can start afresh, I can say what's in my heart?"

"Why would you ever think you couldn't do that?"

"I don't know. The timing always seemed to be—" Jake noticed the light playing off the pendant around Alex's neck. "That's nice, is it new?"

"Yes, it's from a friend."

"What are those stones? They look like diamonds."

"They can't be; it would cost thousands. They're probably crystals."

Jake hesitated. "Friend-friend or boyfriend?"

Alex blushed.

He put his hand over hers. "There it is again."

"There what is?"

"A blush. You did it after I gave you the flowers. I thought it was for me but . . . " He pointed his finger and whirled it around her face. "What's going on, missy?"

"Can't get anything by you, can I? I wasn't going to say anything, but you were wrong about him, and as my best friend, I think you should know it."

"Him? Who him? Not the captain?"

"Yes, the captain. How many guys do you think are interested in me? He's wonderful, Jake. Really sweet and funny, not anything like you thought. Well, maybe a little. He doesn't see me as often as I'd like, but he does call. And he's not married. I'm so crazy about him I think I'm going to burst."

*

Once Alex admitted she'd committed herself to someone, Jake was as supportive as any friend could be. However, he hadn't anticipated how painful it would be to hear her talk so candidly about another man. From somewhere deep inside, he found strength to divert his feelings, for as a true friend the ability to talk about, and accept anything, was part of the deal. Nevertheless, after twenty minutes, he'd had enough. He was crushed and could no longer handle the fact that the only woman who he'd been remotely interested in for years, had given her heart, and by the sound of things, a lot more, to someone else.

In the cold light of what was turning out to be a dreadful day, Jake knew this miserable mess was his fault, and he could've prevented it. If he'd said something sooner, been more affectionate, stopped pussyfooting around, and made a move. If, if, if. He'd never felt so desolate, and urgently needed to get away. "Alex, I'm really sorry. Jeez, I'm like a broken record. But I have to go. I forgot—I have this . . . thing."

"What thing? You invited me here, remember?"

"I know. The, er, meeting just popped back into my mind. I'll call you, make it right, but I have to leave. Er, I'm happy for you, really happy. Remember if you need anything, I'll be there. I just want you to be . . . happy. It's all I ever wanted, take care." He rose from the table, hugged her for longer than usual, and kissed her on the forehead.

*

Alex simply stared, barely able to comprehend the whirlwind that had just occurred. She had never seen Jake so flustered, and she felt sorrow radiating from him. It was almost as if he were saying goodbye. She watched him leave with an overwhelming urge to drag him back. He was at the door when she called out. "See you soon?"

He turned, eyes misted with a look that said he was terribly upset about something. Then he buttoned his overcoat and stepped into the street.

CHAPTER SIXTEEN

When Vera Cruz got into Pete's car at Rome's Fiumicino airport, his mood was dark and somber. The trip had not gone well.

They drove on in silence until they arrived at The Palacio, an opulent establishment on the Via Veneto, oozing old money and the romantic sensibilities of a different era. It was one of Vera Cruz's homes-away-from-home, and always equalized his mood.

As the doorman recognized the car, he stepped forward, and after acknowledging Vera Cruz as Capitan Girgenti, took care of the bag.

*

In the solitude of a familiar room, Vera Cruz unpacked and reviewed the disaster of the previous four days. He'd stayed at a friend's apartment on Jungshahi Street just outside Karachi's airport, where on prior trips she'd proven to be a pleasant diversion. This time, she hadn't shown, not only depriving him of entertainment, but also her useful stewardess hands to recover his flight bag from Abu Dhabi. Now, with the problem still unresolved, his paymaster in Rome had summoned him to discuss the urgent status of that delivery, as well as two other outstanding contracts. Vera Cruz rarely met his agent in a confrontational situation, but at noon, he had the distinct feeling he would be subject to one such circumstance.

*

Pa'vone's bar bustled with the usual crowd vying for one of the sidewalk tables. However, Vera Cruz chose a more secluded wall table, which afforded him a safe back, as well as a clear view of those coming and going. A prime people-watching spot, the bar adjoining The Palacio was frequented by a wealthy female and discretely gay male clientele, who were attracted by the avenue's handsome, beautifully tailored up-and-comers looking for a friend or benefactor. As he sipped cappuccino, Vera Cruz recalled his first months in Rome as one of those desperate young men. That was a lifetime ago, but it amused him to note that assignations of every type still went intentionally unnoticed by Rome's sophisticated romantics.

Feeling a presence overshadowing, Vera Cruz focused to find an imposing figure in mocha silk suit and Prada loafers approaching the table. Preceded by a whiff of expensive cologne and a flourish of hand-sewn kidskin gloves, his agent brushed away non-existent particles from the chair beside the captain and sat. Crossing ankles with as much grace as any portly being can display, Franco placed his gloves on the table and motioned a waiter.

An exquisitely boned young man minced to the table carrying a silver ice bucket containing a bottle of Cristal and, with a lascivious swipe of his tongue over lightly rouged lips, he placed it in the stand beside Franco. The big man tendered no acknowledgement. A second waiter, blond, blue-eyed, and undemonstrative, delivered a single champagne flute, a dozen long-stem strawberries, and a dish of dark chocolate. He received one of Franco's gold-leafed business cards.

As Vera Cruz watched with silent understanding, Franco plunged a chubby, beautifully manicured fingertip into the chocolate. Placing the dollop into his mouth, he savored the bittersweet confection. "Well, capitan," he said, brushing a napkin across lips, "you continue to be the gracious host, but I have to say you disappoint me greatly. My friends in Karachi tell me you are late with several deliveries, including one on which some not so forgiving colleagues are relying and for which you have received an advance of several thousand dollars. I will not ask what happened, as I am in no mood for excuses. Instead, I will say this just once." He took a sip of champagne, letting the tip of his tongue linger on the rim of the glass, so as not to lose a drop of the chilled nectar. "You were chosen to assist our little family with its deliveries because you are a working pilot. And while I appreciate your flying roster may prevent you from accomplishing some of our requests immediately, your seniority affords you ample time to do as we request. That being said, you have three days to make your next delivery, and I will allow you thirty to get my Spider to our UK friends. More importantly, my Semitic associate in the UK informs me that if his organization does not receive its delivery by January first, you will not live to enjoy another Portuguese summer. Do I make myself clear?" A small bead of spittle escaped his lips, and the big man paused to dab at his chin.

Vera Cruz could only look directly at his repulsive, over-indulgent agent for a few seconds, and nodded in the affirmative.

Franco continued. "There is nowhere you can hide, dear capitan. You may think you have all the angles, but believe me, you do not." He paused for effect, to see if Vera Cruz had the audacity to challenge him. When the captain remained silent, Franco resumed. "So my dear, it is said. You know I so hate to play the heavy, my sweet Tayo, but sometimes even my most cherished children need a little encouragement to come back in line. We are still friends, no?" He placed a hand over Vera Cruz's, and squeezed it provocatively. "Now come, dear heart, enjoy a strawberry." Selecting the plumpest of the berries, Franco delicately doused it in the bittersweet essence of cacao and bit off the end. Closing his eyes in a parody of erotic appreciation, he savored the hothouse berry's luscious flavor wrapped in the chocolate's seductive texture. A glossing of chocolate remained on his lip, and running an almost prehensile tongue around his mouth, he removed the last traces of bittersweet.

Watching Franco eat was an obscenity, but as Vera Cruz rose to leave, his agent stirred. "Leaving so soon and you haven't taken a single berry."

"I bought them for you."

"Dear, sweet Tayo, you always remember papa's little weakness."

"It's what I do."

"Yes, quite so. By the by, my driver has placed the next delivery in your hotel room. London expects it within three days. Now run along so I can enjoy my wine and that deliciously fetching young man to my left." Making a gesture signaling the captain was free to leave, Franco motioned for the waiter to join him.

*

Upon entering his hotel room, Vera Cruz couldn't miss the elaborately crated picture propped against the bed. Lifting it with one hand, he estimated its weight at around twenty-five kilos. It was too heavy for what he had in mind, so he decided to un-crate and re-wrap it.

Vera Cruz would never get used to being told what to do, but wasn't about to cross Franco, who though repulsive, was one of the most powerful and well-connected businessmen in Rome. Moreover, Vera Cruz knew that in order to re-establish his credibility he had to get the picture to the UK quickly.

He called Pete. "Just met with Franco—"

"Was he pissed?"

"Wasn't happy, but nothing I can't handle. I've got the painting, needs to be in London in three days."

"That'll screw us up, got a plan?"

"Don't I always?"

"Shoot . . ."

"Get me bubble wrap and parcel tape, not the high-end gallery stuff, something you'd buy from the market. Also, check on the

Spider, Franco says it's ready. I've got thirty days to get it to the UK. Last, my goddamn flight bag. As you probably guessed from the mood this morning, my contact in Karachi went belly up."

"I knew something was biting your ass."

"Well it'll be biting yours too if we don't get that film delivered. I don't have another stew who can do it right now, but find out who we have in Abu Dhabi baggage, kick his useless ass, and tell him to send the fucking bag back to Heathrow. Once it's there, I know exactly who can get it through customs."

"I'm on it, be by with the supplies later."

His second call was to England. "Alex, it's me."

"Me? Who me?"

"Vera Cruz."

"Tayo," she said, finally recognizing his voice. "Hi, sorry, I'm not used to hearing you on the phone. This is the first time you've actually called me; you usually just turn up. Where are you, waiting for me at the airport?"

"Not this time. I just wanted you to know I can't get there, and find out if you liked my gift?"

"Of course I did, but I'd rather have had you deliver it personally."

"I know, but scheduling had other ideas. I'm truly sorry about Paris, but I promise, we'll do it soon. Right now I'm in Rome. Are you working today? Can you come to dinner?"

A small silence followed. "Dinner in Rome? Are you serious?"

"Of course I am. Hop on a flight and stay the night. I need you."

Alex hesitated. "I'm not sure, I'd have to make some calls, change my shifts, get a ticket."

"Don't you think I'm worth the effort?"

"Hmmm . . . now let me think."

"Quit it, Mack, just do it. I'll call you in forty minutes."

Before she had time to say anything, he hung up.

*

With the dazzling light show of a fall sun going down, the Europa flight landed in Rome. And as the aircraft taxied to the stand, Alex stared from her window fantasizing that such a spectacular welcome was an omen of amazing things to come.

Seated up front with an overnight bag, she offloaded first, and while she breezed through immigration and customs, she'd never been to Rome, and had no idea where to go next. She needn't have concerned herself, for as she entered the meeting area, Vera Cruz, looking as strikingly handsome as she remembered, was walking toward her.

Despite having the passion of their last meeting fresh in her thoughts, Alex still didn't know where she fit in Vera Cruz's life, so, playing it safe, she greeted him with a peck on the cheek. In turn, he wrapped her in his arms and planted a kiss on her mouth.

Kindled by a fire she felt totally inappropriate for so public a place, she pushed him away. "Whoa, slow down, we'll get arrested."

"Not here." He grinned, steering her to where his car was waiting. "This is Italy. Romance is part of their religion."

The car had barely left the curb when, like a teenager on a dare, Vera Cruz guided Alex's hand to his lap. He kissed her deep, and it was several minutes before he backed off. "I'm so glad you made it."

"Friends owed me."

"Thank God for friends," he mumbled, nuzzling the contours of her neck.

"Er, Tayo, shouldn't we wait until . . . "

Her resolve evaporated when his tongue made circular motions on her skin, and his hand manipulated the buttons of her blouse and slid effortlessly beneath her bra. She gasped as practiced fingers brought her nipple to fullness, and then, when he leaned down and vigorously sucked her breast, a surprisingly deep clitoral reaction blossomed.

"Tayo, no, really, stop. I'm not sure I can handle this in a car ride from the airport. Besides, the driver can see everything, you'll embarrass him."

"You are so adorably British, I could eat you. But, for now, if it makes you feel better, I'll stop."

"Thank you, I feel better already."

She had barely said the words when his hand slid up the inside of her thigh. "You know you've ruined the driver's day. I'm sure he was expecting a show."

"Then let him go to the Coliseum."

*

It amused Vera Cruz to note her discomfort, particularly as he knew nothing he might do would embarrass Pete. Nevertheless, he could see they were approaching their destination, and complied with Alex's wishes. He grinned as she straightened her disarrayed hair, re-buttoned her blouse, and took up a demure posture for the remaining minutes of the drive. There would be time enough for him to play and more than enough time for him to draw her deeper under his control.

*

At The Palacio, Vera Cruz waved away the approaching porter, grabbed Alex's bag, and hustled her upstairs.

She only managed a fleeting glimpse of the hotel, which seemed impressive, but when he opened the door to his suite, she felt as if she were in a fairytale palace.

Wall sconces cast a warm glow over the sumptuously decorated sitting area, and by a window, a small dining table was romantically set for two, with sparking silver and crystal. A single red rose sat on one of the gold-rimmed plates. And to the table's left, a sideboard held a buffet supper and a bottle of iced champagne. Alex smiled; she was finally learning Vera Cruz's habits.

Looking from the window, she noted that regardless of the late hour, countless couples strolled in the glow of the Via Veneto's lamplight. Wreaths of flowers adorned lamppost tops, their poles striped with gold and silver ribbon. And as far as the eye could see, fairy lights strung along the avenue sparkled bright against a pitch-black sky. The serpentine swayed gently in the occasional breeze, and it seemed as if all Rome was decorated.

Alex rested her head on Vera Cruz's shoulder, and as she let the beauty of Rome flood over her, she decided he was the most romantic man she'd ever met. "It's beautiful, Tayo, thank you so much for sharing this with me."

"I've barely started. Turn around."

*

As Vera Cruz leaned in to kiss her, Alex devoured him. Her aggression pleased him more than he expected, and his body responded. But he wasn't ready to show that weakness in himself, and pushed her back. "Aren't you hungry?"

She glanced at the table. "Not for that." It took seconds for her to shuck her clothes and brush seductively against him.

"Why, Miss Mack, I believe you have the advantage of me."

"Then take off your damn clothes." She unbuckled his belt and pulled him into the bedroom—a dappled cocoon of privacy, with exquisitely scented candles flickering against the walls. "Lie down, let me do some work."

"No, I invited you. We play by my rules."

"Don't we always." She knelt down and took him in her mouth.

Experienced in the ways and moods of women, Vera Cruz couldn't understand how he'd so misjudged Alex's personality. At first, he'd thought her uptight and shy, though her reaction to his advances in the coffee shop had quickly dispelled that idea. Then he'd imagined her inexperienced and needing some persuasion, until her total surrender and enthusiasm for his aggressive lovemaking dissipated that notion. Now, as she systematically teased and tormented his body, she had become more interesting than he'd anticipated. He was eager to see how far she would let him go. He pulled her upright. "That feels good, have you been practicing?"

"No, so let me finish."

"This night is for you." He maneuvered her onto the bed and flipped her over. "Trust me," he whispered in her ear.

A jar of scented oil sat on the nightstand, and he poured a measure into his hands. Then, palms together, he spread the emollient before smoothing it onto her shoulders. With hands kneading softly, and fingers circling light, he felt her muscles relax. Spreading more oil, he worked slowly this way and that, down her back. She had been tense, but he felt her total surrender beneath his silken touch. And with practiced hands, he continued his fluid caress about her buttocks. Up and out, with gentle strokes. Around and down, he smoothly explored. Then a lubricated finger slid between. He knew from her reaction that she'd never experienced this chapter of anyone's erotic agenda. But with gentle insistence, he entered the darkness within.

With ears attuned to her moaning, Vera Cruz fingered back and forth, and when he felt her arc toward him, he repositioned and slid inside her.

She gasped as his penis entered her body.

"Am I hurting you?" he whispered.

"No, it just feels odd."

"Back up into me a little."

He continued his fluid penetration, until he felt her relax into his rhythm. Then he reached beneath her.

With silken fingers circling her clitoris, she came to an explosive release. And as she screamed his name, Vera Cruz knew she would do anything he asked.

*

The lovers emerged from the bathroom wearing only the hotel's thick perfumed robes. His hand was light as kisses on the back of her neck, and his blatant sensuality kept Alex's senses reeling. She was irretrievably lost and undeniably in love, and when his lips brushed light on hers, a moan escaped her throat. Melding into his body, still hard with desire and unspent passion, she wondered what inexplicable something caused him to so swiftly ignite a sexual firestorm within her. And though she was more than a little frightened by his power over her, she wanted to stay where she was, lose herself in his depth-less green eyes, feel his lips on hers, and have his body make sensible thought fly out the window.

She wasn't sure when they collapsed into bed or what time they went to sleep. But she was groggy when the ringing phone woke her. Blinking sleep from her eyes, and trying to avoid the blinding sun streaming through half-open drapes, she reached across to ask him to stop the noise. He wasn't there. Confused, Alex picked up the phone. "Hello?"

"It's me."

"Where are you?"

"At crew reporting."

"You have got to be joking. I fly halfway round the world to see you, and you ditch me for work?"

"Can't be helped."

"Yes, it can. Tell them to go to hell. You can't be the only pilot they have on staff."

"It's my job, Alex."

"Well, screw your job, this is—"

"Don't make me feel any worse than I do. I'll make it up, you know I will. Don't I make you feel good? Can't you tell how much I care for you? But I have a job to do."

"It's not fair."

"I know, but look, the hotel is paid for, have breakfast, get the concierge to book you a tour, he'll add anything you want to my tab. I'll see you back in London in a few days."

"A few days! Why aren't you coming back this evening?"

"Sorry, baby, I go where I'm told. Please bear with me. When I get back, it will be that much more fun."

"More fun than last night?"

"Guarantee it."

"Ouch, I'm not sure I can handle that."

"You will, I'll teach you."

"I think you've taught me quite enough already."

"I haven't even started."

"My God, who are you, and what planet are you from?"

"For that information, you'll have to stick around. You will, won't you?"

"If you want me to."

"I want you to."

"I miss you already."

"I know."

She giggled at his confidence. "So what happens now, you'll call me or what?"

"I'll call, soon. By the way, a driver will pick you up around four; you're taking Al Italia home."

"You organized a flight for me?"

"Couldn't leave my best girl completely stranded, could I?"

"Thank you."

"Oh, Alex, one thing. Could you do me a favor?"

"Name it."

"A friend of mine came to Rome and purchased a picture, but when it arrived at the airport, it wasn't suitably packaged for shipment. I said I'd repack it and carry it over today. However, now I'm going to be in Cairo. Would you mind taking it?"

"What about—"

"Customs? Don't worry about that. The receipt for purchase is taped to the back, and you won't have to take it home—my friend will be waiting at Heathrow arrivals to collect it."

"No problem. When will I see you again?"

"Can't talk any more, baby, I'm being paged. Next time we meet, I'll find an extra special way to thank you. I'll call you, okay?"

"Okay, take care. I love—" She was talking to dead air.

*

Alex took her time over brunch, people-watched at Pa'vone's, and followed that with two hours in the hotel's spa. She returned to her room as the front desk informed her a car was waiting to take her to the airport.

In the lobby, she was somewhat embarrassed to find the driver who'd witnessed the sexually charged ride between her and Vera Cruz the night before. However, though she nodded, a blank look of non-recognition stared back.

*

It was raining when the flight landed at Heathrow, and looking from the window she could see several flights converging on what appeared to be fully occupied gates. The Al Italia flight, being a night stop scheduled to depart first thing in the morning, would normally position close to the terminal building. However, for some reason—and Alex could only assume it was the volume of incoming flights—the aircraft parked a considerable distance from the terminal.

She was one of the first to disembark, and looking through the gangway window, was grateful she didn't have to lug the picture in the rain. That was, until she exited onto the pier and saw the half-mile trek to arrivals stretched out before her. The picture wasn't heavy, just awkward, and she found herself constantly adjusting her overnight bag to compensate for its bulk. Frustrated with herself for not clarifying the size of the thing before agreeing to transport it, she was about to begin dragging it unceremoniously across the floor when a man tapped her on the shoulder.

"Looks like you need some help," he said. "Would you like to share my cart?"

He looked vaguely familiar, but as airlines have many regular passengers, she dismissed the thought. "Thanks so much, I should have asked for one to meet me, but I had no idea this thing would be so awkward."

"Looks like a painting, is it heavy?"

"Not really, it'll balance on what you've got there. I can carry my bag."

"Wouldn't think of it," he answered, repositioning his two large cases and taking the picture. "These calibrators might be too delicate for loaders to throw about, but the cases are plenty sturdy. I'll lay this one flat, and you can dump your bag on top."

Trundling precariously toward the immigration and customs checkpoints, Alex and her new friend moved quickly through British passport control. However, in negotiating the desk, the picture caught on the barrier, and it and her bag crashed to the ground.

"Damn thing," she mumbled, reaching for the picture.

"Okay, miss," responded the control point security guard. "I got it." He smiled and placed the picture back on the cart.

Alex and her gallant friend parted company in the baggage hall, where she transferred her belongings to another cart and set off for the "nothing to declare" section. She couldn't shake the feeling of being watched, but hauling a large picture would naturally garner some attention. Vera Cruz said it was of no real value. Nevertheless, should she be stopped, she had the picture's receipt ready for customs.

As the crowd streamed past empty examination tables, there appeared to be no officers on duty. However, as Alex was halfway through the area, a disembodied voice told everybody to stop. In doing so, she ran into another passenger's cart and again, the picture hit the floor with a resounding thud. She hauled it back onto the cart as the disembodied voice became three customs officers. One stood at the exit as a second pointed to a scruffy young man at the far side of the crowd. He shuffled toward the examination tables, looking decidedly worse for some sort of narcotic. In passing Alex's cart, he clipped the picture's corner and sent it sliding across the floor. The third officer stopped its forward motion with his foot.

Alex stepped forward to retrieve the picture and recognized the customs officer. "Oh, hi, Steve. Thanks for stopping it."

"Alex, hi yourself. Hope this thing isn't valuable, 'cos it's taking a real beating?"

She smiled at Steve, who had on a couple of occasions let her slip through controls with an extra bottle of wine. "It's not. But let me give you a tip, never buy a picture abroad, no matter how much you like it or how cheap it is. This piece of junk is more trouble than it's worth. If I get it home without putting my foot through it, it'll be a miracle."

"Any booze today?"

"No time. I only just made the flight hauling this thing."

"Know what you mean, those staff passes can leave you cutting it fine."

As he lifted the picture back onto the cart, she offered him the receipt. "Want to check this?"

"Nah, I trust you. You on tomorrow?"

"Late shift."

"Me too. Want to get a coffee?"

"Maybe, let's see how things go. I'll call the office if I can make it."

It was well known Alex didn't date staff, so he nodded and let her proceed onto the arrivals concourse.

When the doors hissed to a close behind her, Alex waited a few seconds to give anyone looking for her time to approach. At the same time, she checked names on the limo-drivers boards to see if one of them was for her. Neither appeared to be the case, so she decided to take the picture home and wait for Vera Cruz to call and tell her what to do with it.

It took several minutes to negotiate the tightly packed crowd and exit the terminal. And as she negotiated the first curb ramp, a striking redhead approached her.

"You Alex?" she demanded.

"Yes, why?"

"That's my picture."

"Hallelujah. It's awkward, you take the—"

The woman rudely snatched the cart and pushed it away without even a thank you.

Alex resisted the urge to say something; she was simply relieved to hand over the picture. But as she watched the woman trundle to a Range Rover and gently place the picture in a frame carrier at back, she recalled Vera Cruz saying it was valued at less than eighty pounds. The reverence with which the redhead handled the painting appeared odd. Nevertheless, she was too tired to give it serious thought.

As she sunk into her car, exhaustion kicked in. Not the sort caused by lugging a piece of junk across a continent, but the good, contended kind you get from a night of passion with someone you're crazy about. And despite dwelling in the privacy of her thoughts, Alex remembered what actions had prompted such tiredness. She blushed, for some people might think her not quite decent. But she was young and adventurous and felt nothing between lovers should be off limits. On balance, she cared nothing for what anyone else thought. Vera Cruz made her feel deliciously alive. And if she could spend her life repeating their nights of uninhibited carnality, it was well worth how lousy she currently felt.

CHAPTER SEVENTEEN

When Vera Cruz called Red, she wasn't complimentary about Alex. But petty jealousy wasn't something that remotely bothered him. His primary interest was the picture's safe arrival. And when Red confirmed that, he hung up the phone and shifted his focus. It was the pompous fat man that bothered him.

Despite Franco's implication, Vera Cruz had never had difficulty completing the tasks on his schedule, and the Italian's Spider from Rome to Folkestone was next. And as he thought about how much he despised Franco and his lectures about "the capitan" not being in control of his own life, he was truly irritated. It didn't matter that the obsequious reptile wielded power because of the people with whom he shared his body. Vera Cruz had simply had enough of fat cats with bad attitudes, haranguing him about things of which they had little knowledge. But it wouldn't be for much longer.

It took him a week to set up the trip from Italy to the UK, ensuring he avoided high profile cities and towns. And Alex was essential to the plan. She'd not only be a pleasant diversion, but if she was to help with his flight bag, she had to be deeply entrenched in wrongdoing, and firmly under his control.

CHAPTER EIGHTEEN

It had been a strange day for Alex. She'd seen Jake twice, even called after him and waved. But he'd looked straight through her with no acknowledgement. They'd been friends for so long and had shared so much, that this sudden indifference from him bothered her. Needing to find out what was wrong, she did something she said she'd never do. She called him at the Special Branch office.

Speaking briefly to Eddie Barstow, the seeming instigator of all their misunderstandings, Alex was curtly told Jake was working undercover and couldn't be reached. That statement alone worried her, because no matter in what Jake had previously been embroiled, he'd always managed to say a quick hello or pass back a message.

*

As another night alone left her with the distinct feeling that the two most important men in her life were avoiding her, Alex attempted to put the strange triangle of her life into some sort of perspective.

Vera Cruz was a beautiful mysterious creature she'd known for only a few weeks. He drove her to distraction with his erratic comings and goings, but took her to several kinds of heaven when they were together. They were undoubtedly on the same page physically—though she could never admit to anyone what extraordinarily erotic things he did to her. However, emotionally, he was evasive and secretive. And she had no real idea who he was, or whether she figured in his life.

Jake was her rock, her closest friend, someone whose sensitive caring she'd treasured for years. They were mentally closer than many married couples, and she dearly missed his counsel. His humor and quiet strength sustained her, and she always thought they'd be friends forever. And while there was nothing physical between them, she now realized why his supposedly forgotten meeting had him walking out on her at Java Julia's. He wanted them to be a couple. Alex cursed. She was in the middle of a mess, and all she wanted was to talk to him and explain her feelings.

When the phone rang, she expected it was finally Jake.

"Hi, baby."

She squelched a disappointed sigh. "Tayo, hi, I wasn't expecting you."

"You have someone else in your life?"

"Yes . . . er . . . no . . . not exactly."

"That makes it clear, what's wrong?"

"Something to do with work. I'll figure it out. Forget it. How are you? Where are you? Am I going to see you soon?"

"Perhaps."

"Christ, not more wait-and-see games." He'd picked a bad moment for another mystery. "Come on, Tayo, this is wearing a bit thin. I sit by the phone waiting for your calls, and then you arrive out of nowhere with no thoughts for whether I have other plans. Next thing I know, it's wham bam thank you ma'am, and you're gone. You have me trail you all the way to Rome. We have sex, and before I can wash the sweat off my belly, you're off into the wide blue yonder. I don't want to be some chick you call, screw, and dump. Who are you, Tayo? What are you? Engaged, married, what? I'm sick of playing second fiddle to . . . something! So tell me. I'm all ears. Where do you want me next? Should I bother bringing clothes? How about I lie prostrate and naked somewhere until you get around to me? Whatever I want, it's going to be all about you. And about now, I feel sure I'm not going to like what you're about to tell me."

"After that little speech, I'm not sure, either. Maybe I should hang up and let you take out whatever's bugging you on someone else."

His tone had an uncompromising edge she'd not heard before.

"No, Tayo, don't go, please don't go. I'm sorry, I had a really bad day, and I think a friend is sick and I can't get hold of him. Don't hang up, I need you."

"You're going to behave?"

"I promise."

"Okay, as long as you accept I can't be there as often as you'd like. I thought we sorted this out, because I was under the impression you understood and were all right with it. If things have changed, tell me right now, and we'll say goodbye on a good note."

"No! No goodbyes. I'm sorry, truly sorry. I want you in my life."

"Remember you said that. I don't want to have to remind you that it was you who asked me to stay. Now enough hysterics, I don't like it. I said I'd make it up to you."

"I know, I know, but I've been so lonely—"

"What do you think about a trip across Europe?"

There was a short silence. "Across where?"

"Europe. A friend who lives in Folkestone bought an Alpha Romeo Spider in Rome. He asked me to drive it back to the UK for him. Want to come along for the ride?"

CHAPTER NINETEEN

Although late November, the day was warm and bright as Alex arrived at Fiumicino airport. Moving swiftly through controls, she eagerly anticipated being with her lover. She'd slept fitfully the night before, and was unsure whether her anxiety was because doubts and fears had begun to set in about Vera Cruz or because she was thrilled at the prospect of spending two weeks of days, and nights, with the man she loved. Her mind had been abuzz with the prospect of getting inside his head, and decided that while he hadn't actually said so, such an intimate excursion clearly indicated a turning point in their relationship.

She was brought heavily down to earth when a distant, and only moderately affectionate, Vera Cruz greeted her.

For a moment, she was confused, wondering whether she'd made the right decision in coming to Rome. Then she looked at him and recognized the fault was hers. Her intense longing for him had created an expectation no mortal could satisfy.

As Vera Cruz pulled into the heaving mass of traffic leaving the airport, Alex put a hand on his thigh. "You seem tense, is everything okay?" she asked.

"I just hate crawling through this airport traffic."

"Aren't you used to it? After all, you do it every day to get to work."

"I usually have a driver."

Alex smiled. She'd learned something new about him. Then she remembered. "Not the guy who took me to Al Italia."

"His name is Pete. He's been with me for years."

"Oh God, he saw us making out."

"Don't worry, you're not the first."

"What?"

"Alex, I'm a man, not a priest."

"I know, but—"

"But nothing, be realistic. You must know I see other women."

"Then, but now—"

"Baby, please, we just met, don't rush things."

"Okay, sorry, but I want you to know, I'm not seeing anyone else."

"I know."

Alex wasn't sure how to respond, and a wave of uneasiness flooded over her. Then, when Vera Cruz passed the exit for Rome and turned toward the coast road, she knew there'd be no rekindling of their passionate night at The Palacio. They were obviously returning to the UK immediately.

*

With business, then urban districts falling quickly behind them, the Spider advanced up the coast road. And as the volume of traffic thinned, there appeared a perceptible easing of the tense atmosphere engulfing them. That was until the Spider's speed dramatically increased.

Alex had little experience with foreign motorists. And Italian drivers did nothing to bolster her confidence, as multiple-passenger mopeds and engine-racing compact cars weaved in and out at high speed. Moreover, while she knew fast cars were one of Vera Cruz's passions, she didn't entirely approve of his support of the racetrack mentality.

"At this rate," she said, clutching the door rest, "we'll be home in two days."

"Need to make up some time."

"Make up time? I thought we had two weeks."

"About that—"

"Jesus, Tayo, don't tell me—things have changed."

"I've been assigned a flight from Gatwick on December fourth."

"The fourth? You have to be ready to fly on the fourth?"

"0730 departure."

"That means we have less than a week. Can you even do it in that time?"

"Sure, if we make fewer stops."

"Well, isn't that a bitch. I suppose I can sit cross-legged for ten hours at a stretch."

"Excuse me?"

"Nothing. It just seems that where you and I are concerned, flying will always come first."

"I know it seems that way, baby, but it won't be for much longer. I'm working on a retirement plan."

"Does it include me?"

He smiled and took her hand. "Don't rush things, okay?"

As the coast road stretched ahead, Vera Cruz looked in his rearview. Nothing was following so he reduced speed.

*

The Spider remained alone for miles, eating up the twisted coastal byway that ran atop a cliff's edge. Whenever he drove such roads, he was reminded of Pete's predecessor, Danilo, and their disastrous end in Portugal. For it was on a similar road they'd been intercepted by the authorities. Like the shelf on which that particular road ran, this one was cut by loose-stoned exits, pitched at dizzying angles, running right down to the sea. But this time he didn't anticipate having to plummet down one to escape. Today, he could relax and look down on the villages with their fishing boats moored tight at the water's edge. And for someone who'd never had time to look at the countryside he traversed, he felt mellow.

But was his serenity due to his retiring from the madness in which he'd been living for more years than he cared to remember? Or was it something else? As he looked across at Alex, wide-eyed and innocent in many ways, he wondered if she had brought about such feelings. He couldn't remember meeting anyone so fresh and guileless, and he'd never tolerated any other woman questioning his comings and goings. Was she making him soft? Might his feelings for her be different from all the others?

The small silver sports car sped on through foothills bejeweled with villas glowing rosy pink and warm terracotta, fronted by approach roads with seemingly impossible inclines. And where the hills were workable, terrace upon terrace of olive trees and grapevines hung dormant. Moreover, as the soft light of the November sun etched deep shadows into the mountains, the muted greens and fading tans of season's end foliage stood in sharp contrast to the bright blue of a cloudless sky. In the beauty of the moment, lost in something he'd never experienced before, Vera Cruz reached for Alex's hand. Should he let her into his life?

*

By mid-afternoon, enjoying the contemplative, strangely calming journey, Vera Cruz asked Alex if she was ready for a break. She was, and as he knew several restaurants on the road north, he pulled into one of his favorites outside Livorno.

The Trattoria Oreste not only had a spectacular ocean overview, but also allowed its patrons to share the family garden. And though it was late autumn, the warmth of the sun and the mildness of the sea breeze had encouraged several couples to dine al fresco. One could either sit on the terraced patio at white wrought iron tables under elegant purple and gold canopies or throw a couple of the trattoria's brightly colored blankets on the grassy slope overlooking the ocean. Vera Cruz knew what would most appeal to Alex.

*

Nothing was said as they came to a halt, and while it was true the trip north had lightened Vera Cruz's mood, when Alex left the car for a bathroom break she had the feeling something was still weighing heavily on his mind. It was several minutes after she returned that he appeared with a picnic basket and blankets. Leading Alex to the overlook, he laid one of the thick covers on the ground, and as soon as they were seated he draped his arm around her shoulder and tenderly kissed her neck.

"I'm sorry I've been evasive, Alex, I guess I really needed a few miles under my belt to shake off work."

She giggled. "You're forgiven because I adore picnics. It almost makes up for you being such a pig."

"That's a bit extreme; I thought my behavior only moderately boorish."

"Nice play on words, Captain, but a clever comeback isn't going to get you out of a proper apology. I expect big things when we get to the hotel."

Vera Cruz smiled, inclined his head, and touched his heart, lips, and forehead like a Bedouin to his master. "Your wish is my command, O pale one."

She cuffed him around the shoulder. "Fool, let's eat."

With a blanket tented around them like a couple of kids, they spent the next hour munching on the selection of meats, fruit, and cheeses from the picnic basket. However, by the time they got to the pignoli cookies and shakerato for which the trattoria was famous, Vera Cruz reminded Alex they needed to get back on the road and travel a few more miles before nightfall. Pouting and protesting, she wanted to stay where she was, but he pulled her to her feet, flicked her rump, and pushed her giggling toward the car.

As they motored toward Genoa, Alex encountered a new and tantalizing softness in Vera Cruz, and having his body so close to hers inspired her to mischief. Tracing small circles on the inside of his thigh, she came dangerously close to arousing actions not conducive to safe driving.

"Hey," he said, playfully swatting her. "You want us over the cliff?"

"I want us over something."

"Then you're going to have to wait."

"Umm, promises, promises."

"Behave, Miss Mack, this road is not the only thing that's dangerous."

The following hours proved some of the most carefree either of them had spent; they debated politics, laughed about the inconsistencies of airline life, and were completely enamored with each other. And as night fell, they pulled into the elegant Bristol Hotel in Genoa.

Check-in was somewhat of a challenge for Alex, who'd been waiting all day to get her hands on Vera Cruz's body. Bristling with anticipation, she hustled him to their suite. He had barely closed the door before she was naked and demanding he make good on his promise.

He needed little encouragement, and after unceremoniously depositing his clothes in a trail to the bed with no kissing, caressing, or foreplay, he pushed her onto her back and entered her. He was forceful, but she was very wet and quickly adjusted to him. And as their rhythm flowed, and that sweet spot of nerves connected with the deliberate friction of his high-ridged penis, Alex wallowed in a state of electrifying bliss. She was entirely under his spell as a million feathers brushed her skin, and when he slowed his thrust, to match the rotation of her hips, she begged for more. Alex had no idea why he made something she'd done a thousand times so devastating to her senses. She simply concentrated on his delicate friction and floated in a half-life.

Then he paused, and quieting her disappointed moan with kisses, he whispered, "Put your legs over my shoulders."

As Alex repositioned her legs, he reached places so deep she gasped. But he felt exquisite. And when she tightened her muscles to drag the life from him, he matched her movement, producing sensations she had no idea were possible.

They moved together in perfect rhythm, but he was all power and outpaced her. And when she felt him quickening, she was lost in that moment of sublime euphoria, and raked her fingernails across his back. She was so focused on her goal, she barely noticed him change position. Until he bit down on her engorged nipples, and her pain and pleasure tracks aligned, exploding her body into rolling undulations of transcendent misery. And as she gyrated wildly in an attempt to drag him deeper, he bit down on her again. A second orgasm exploded. Deep and more centered than the first, she surrendered to his domination, hovering somewhere just below consciousness. She reveled in the little death he brought her. And when she could take no more, she screamed his name and fainted to black.

As Vera Cruz drove on into her seemingly lifeless body, salt sweat dripped onto her breasts, deep rising and falling, flushed crimson with sated desire. And then he moaned, a deep primeval noise from his very soul, and settled silently atop her.

Alex lay spent, her every fiber screaming for mercy, tears flowing. But they were not tears of her deliberate making, but an outpouring of emotion over which she had no control.

For several tranquil minutes, she felt his body heavy and silent, and when he moved off her, joy disappeared from her soul.

"Where are you going?" she mumbled, throat parched.

"You okay?" he whispered. "I thought I'd lost you for a minute."

Reaching up, she traced sweat beads on his beautiful face. "You certainly know how to pay your debts."

"It was my pleasure."

"How do you make me feel so loved and so lost at the same time?"

"My intention is simply to make you feel good."

"But you do so much more. You've taken over my mind, my heart, my very soul. And it feels so right; I want to be with you, forever."

"Forever is a long time." He pecked her on the nose.

"So where are you going?"

"Shower of course."

"You don't want to just lie here and be close for while?"

"No."

"Can I come in the shower with you?"

"Not this time. You sleep a little, something tells me you're not used to my kind of payback."

His jade green eyes mesmerized, but Alex saw no emotion there. He'd just made aggressive love to her and within seconds appeared fully recovered. And when she ran her hand over his chest, there was no wildly thumping heart, no irregular breathing, no discernible emotion at all. "What are you, a machine?"

"Something like that."

"But you do eat, right?"

He smiled. "Yes, I eat."

"Then I'll order dinner. It'll be ready by the time you get out the shower. Now be really quick because I'm famished."

"The proper exercise will do that."

"Monster . . . "

He caught the pillow she threw at him and lobbed it back.

CHAPTER TWENTY

Standing on the balcony sipping coffee, Alex watched Vera Cruz interact with the hotel's staff. He seemed so open and relaxed in his dealings with strangers it made his oft-time reticence toward her puzzling. She smiled, wondering how much of himself he'd ever reveal to her, and whether it mattered. All she was certain of was that they'd spent another night fulfilling her most secret sexual fantasies leaving her feeling that their actions had formed a special bond between them. She didn't quite know where that bond might lead, or why the thought of any such commitment should manifest itself now, and she didn't care. It had been a huge step to admit she would be forever devoted to him, but in relinquishing control of her body and mind, she'd never felt better. Alex knew she'd found the man with whom she wanted to spend the rest of her life.

As she packed the last of her things, she noticed Vera Cruz had removed every vestige of his being there. His things were gone from the bathroom. He'd tidied the sitting room, and folded away every towel. It seemed he had some sort of Invisible Man, neat freak quirk, and that tiny telltale insecurity endeared him to her. And as she thought of who endeared who to whom, or who was being insecure about what, the thought of being without him consumed her. A tear slid from her eye, evidence of her own lack of confidence, and Alex berated herself. She was determined not to succumb to girlish emotions, knowing that an intelligent, independent woman shouldn't base her future on cute personality traits, or a man's ability to satisfy her sexual desires. Nevertheless, no matter what the rationalization, she was so addicted to his particular brand of carnality that she wasn't sure how she was going to cope after they parted in Folkestone. As tears rolled down her cheek, Vera Cruz entered the room.

Smiling to himself, he approached and wrapped her in his arms. He'd seen this intense emotional outpouring before, and it was easy to persuade her to tell him what was wrong. Then, with eyes honest and sincere, his touch gentle and comforting, he assured her he cared too much to see her sad and promised never to leave her. Alex was left with no doubts about what he was saying.

CHAPTER TWENTY-ONE

There was a marked absence of traffic as Vera Cruz pulled into Calais, and when he wound down his window, the normally bustling seaport sat ominously quiet.

Alex woke as the bone-chilling damp of drifting Channel mist entered the car. "Did we arrive?"

"Didn't mean to wake you."

"Where are we?"

"Calais. I have to check crossing times."

"The ferry? Isn't the Chunnel quicker?"

"Maybe, but it's not my style. I'm going to cruise the parking lot and see if I can find anyone about."

"Everything's closed. What are you looking for?"

"Crossing information. It might look deserted, but there are always security guards on duty."

"Security guards? I know this is the narrowest point, but do they expect someone might swim to England?"

"You'd be surprised what a desperate someone might do."

"So cruise away, but close the window, it's freezing."

Having passed through Calais several months earlier, Vera Cruz was familiar with its high-season security procedures. Now he needed to find someone with whom he could discuss the port's current readiness level. He knew there was always someone not quite happy about the way things were run, and he had a knack of honing in on, and drawing information from, such people. The captain found his informant manning a distant security booth at the ferry-ramp exit.

Pulling to a stop, Vera Cruz got out of the car and in fluent French engaged the guard in conversation.

From the beginning of their exchange, it was obvious the guard didn't see many people during his shift, for he offered a string of garrulous responses to Vera Cruz's questions about terminal operations. Moreover, when the captain indicated he was a ferry enthusiast, touring the ports of Europe, the guard was more than happy to share his opinion on the size and effectiveness of Calais's security operations. The guard also mentioned loads had been light for the past few days, and a simple phone call worker to worker would reserve a berth. Vera Cruz accepted the guard's suggestion, and after patiently listening to several laborious minutes of griping about the politics of terminal management, the captain had the information he was seeking.

*

No words were exchanged as Vera Cruz got back in the car, but Alex's enigmatic smile indicated she had learned a little something about him. In addition to English and Italian, he, like her, spoke fluent French. That information might appear to have no relevance in the larger scheme of things, but in Alex's mind, it opened a whole new line of conversation. There was no mistaking that Vera Cruz had referred to Alex as his wife, and she wondered whether something she'd only dreamed about was happening.

As Vera Cruz headed back the way they had come, Alex placed a hand on his thigh, but there was no acknowledgement from him. She frowned, not only because she recognized the same dark disposition she'd witnessed outside Rome, but because despite being near the end of their journey, in which she'd expected to learn everything about him, she still knew very little. With no idea how to broach the subject of his flip-flopping moods, let alone question him about the possibility of marriage, she withdrew her hand.

As they drove along, Alex stared into gloom beyond the car's window. And the impenetrable grey pall did nothing to ease her desperation. Under normal circumstances, being near the water would lift her spirits, but not tonight. With her mind a catalog of questions, and her heart a confusion of emotions, she couldn't help recalling what he'd said about expecting too much of him. But was her need to know about him and his life unreasonable? Why should she be available to him, without question, as and when his timetable dictated, while she was barely permitted to ask questions of him? Why should she remain quiet and play the dutiful girlfriend, wife, whatever, while he was free to travel wherever, with whomever he pleased?

And then it struck her. Setting aside sex, when she could demand and get what she wanted, at no other time did anything she did matter. It was his agenda, on his terms. He called all the shots, and should things not go according to his plans, it was she who was wracked with guilt. It was patently clear he was adept at avoiding answering personal questions, and Alex wondered if she'd ever penetrate the cloud of secrecy that surrounded him.

*

Vera Cruz was in no mood for conversation. His preference would have been an immediate sail followed by a quiet night in Folkestone. However, with the rolling Channel mist engulfing Calais, he resigned himself to boarding the morning ferry.

He knew exactly where to find safe accommodations, and heading back to the center of town, he wound through Calais's narrow streets to the Hotel Port-Sur-Mer.

Parking the Spider in a small lot next to the hotel's restaurant, Vera Cruz linked Alex's arm and they each took a bag. Their closeness had little effect against the frigid damp and after moving quickly through the swirling fog, they entered the hotel's beamed and wainscoted lobby. A welcoming cocoon of warmth quickly enveloped them, and while Alex headed directly to the roaring fire, Vera Cruz attended the front desk. There, the hotel's owner, Yves Gerard, extended his old friend a boisterous greeting.

*

Alex heard their exchange, but witnessing so unfamiliar a gesture from her lover merely reinforced how little she knew about him. All she was certain of, she was tired and hungry and her hands and face were like blocks of ice. Her immediate need was to return a semblance of normality to her extremities. It didn't take long for the roaring fire to render her toasty, and as she turned to give a final boost of warmth to her back, she noticed Vera Cruz incline his head toward her. Curiosity got the better of her and she joined the men.

"What are you two up to?" she asked Vera Cruz, trying not to sound possessive.

"Attempting to pursuade Yves and his wife to join us for dinner. Alex, let me introduce you to an old friend, Yves Gerard."

"Mademoiselle Alex, very nice to meet you." He planted the customary kisses on Alex's cheeks. "Welcome to my humble house, I hope you will be comfortable."

"I'm sure I will, and you must join us for dinner. From the sound of things you and Tayo have some catching up to do."

"Regrets, mademoiselle, the house will be full tonight and I have a wedding party taking over my restaurant. Maybe next time."

Alex looked at Vera Cruz who nodded. "That sounds good. I always like to hear there will be a next time."

"So, my friends, your key. As always for Tayo, the admiral's suite." Yves handed Vera Cruz a key, and with a measure of understanding only acceptable between friends, he winked.

Vera Cruz smiled. "As you're full, will there be a table available for dinner?"

"For you, of course. Say, fifteen minutes. I'll make sure Jean-Paul seats you at your usual table."

Alex followed Vera Cruz up a burnished oak staircase past original oil paintings of seascapes and sailing ships, and they entered an expansive bed/sitting room overlooking the wharf. Decorated in the style of a high-ranking seafarer's home in the early 1800s, it had a preponderance of dark wood, making it as welcoming and cozy as the hotel's lobby.

"This is a beautiful room, Tayo, but I'm a bit miffed about the 'as always,' and 'usual table' business. Do you bring all your lovers here?"

Vera Cruz pulled Alex into his arms. "Is that a problem for you?"

"How many?"

"Dozens."

"No, seriously, are there notches on the bedpost?"

"Alex, stop. It is what it is. You're here now and that's all that matters." He kissed her deep and hard and she began to relax, he pulled away. "Now freshen up, we have dinner waiting."

"You certainly know how to snap out of the mood."

"Part of my charm. Now hurry, I'm starving."

*

By the size of the milling crowd, wedding guests were arriving at The Bounty. However, Jean-Paul, the restaurant's Maître d', called them forward and seated them at a secluded corner table. A bottle of Dom Pérignon, courtesy of Yves, was waiting.

They were left alone to enjoy dinner until Yves approached them with dessert. Bowing courteously to Alex, the worried looking restaurateur placed the dishes. "Mademoiselle," he said. "Excuse my intrusion, but Captain Vera Cruz has a phone call from his crew control that cannot wait."

"Good grief, Tayo," snapped Alex. "How do they always know where to find you?"

"It's my job."

"I know, I know, business comes first. Well, I'm telling you now, I'm probably going to eat this entire crème brûlée and I'm certainly drinking the rest of the champagne."

Vera Cruz pecked Alex on the forehead and followed Yves to his office.

It was no hardship for Alex to eat dessert and sip champagne inside a reproduction of a sixteenth-century merchantman galleon. And without the distraction of Vera Cruz, she was able to study the room, full of nautical treasures. Travel in all its forms had always fascinated her, and when it had a historical tie-in, she was mesmerized. Clearly, she was not the only patron eager to peruse the décor close up, and when she asked a waiter for clarification on a certain item, she was told to feel free to walk around.

Alex happily wandered the room. With so many things to look at, she all but forgot Vera Cruz's absence—until he returned, grimmer than she'd ever seen him.

"Is everything all right?" she asked, setting down her champagne.

"Fine," he replied. "We finished here?"

When they returned to their room, Vera Cruz was no longer in the mood to talk, neither was he in the mood for anything else. For the first time since they began sharing each other's bodies, he did not approach Alex, but continued to display the darkness she dreaded. She wasn't sure if she should say or do anything to try to bring him around. Then it dawned on her. They would soon be at their destination and if his conversation with the dock guard meant anything, it appeared he was going to miss "his wife" as much as she would miss him. With that thought to comfort her, Alex drifted into sleep.

*

Vera Cruz was restless. There had been no phone call from crew control; the ruse had been Yves's way of relaying a disturbing development. A class of cadet customs inspectors, eager to make names for themselves, would be manning the docks the following day. That notwithstanding, Vera Cruz felt his bases were covered. Should anyone watching him be looking for a car occupied by a single male driver, they were out of luck. His decision to bring Alex along should divert any immediate attention he alone might have drawn.

CHAPTER TWENTY-TWO

When the Spider arrived at the ferry terminal at 5:45 a.m., lines were building and ferries loading. Pulling to the Folkestone booking booth, Vera Cruz learned the security guard he'd befriended the night before had reserved him a berth. However, he wasn't particularly pleased when the clerk loudly announced to all within earshot, "François' friend has arrived!" Nevertheless, they moved quickly from the ticketing area to the snaking line at the immigration and customs checkpoints.

At immigration, clearance cards were punched and passports checked with no more ado than a regular day. And at customs, Vera Cruz smiled confidently as two cadets cast envious eyes over the Alpha Romeo. There didn't appear to be the excess of inspectors he'd anticipated, and the cadets only cursorily checked the car's interior. There was no sign of a sniffer dog or a machine which might detect the Spider's cargo.

Vera Cruz drove unchallenged onto the ferry and into a parking spot, and once the car was safely tethered, he and Alex went up top where the Channel's murky early-morning precipitation dripped cold and depressing. Not having taken a ferry before, Alex wanted to see what was going on. Grabbing hold of the vessel's slimy rails, she leaned over to watch the maneuvering it took to get the ferry underway.

Vera Cruz, on the other hand, repeatedly checked his watch and paced impatiently. By ten minutes past six, the ferry had still not dropped all its lines, and as the clock ticked inexorably on, Vera Cruz worried his luck was about to run out. Then he heard a commotion below.

Joining Alex at the rail, he saw the raised voices belonged to stevedores wrestling with the mooring lines. It appeared they were playing out a pantomime in which one of their number scurried back and forth, gesticulating and screaming at someone in the ferry's wheelhouse. And following the performance back, it was evident that despite cursing, kicking, and cajoling, none of the company was able to release the last of the ferry's lines. Then an oil-smeared goliath, armed with a gigantic wrench, began beating the winch casing into submission.

*

From the boat's distance, Alex could see the sweat beading on his body as the wrench arced over his head onto the mechanism. And as the resounding clang of metal upon metal gave way to a string of colorful profanities, he prevailed. The rope line quietly disconnected, slithering submissively beneath the turbid water. And with a triumphant wail of the vessel's steam-filled siren, the throbbing behemoth departed the dock.

The few passengers on board descended below to take refuge in the ferry's main salon. However, while Alex was able to shake the moisture from her coat, it was harder to unsettle the chill from her bones. Vera Cruz noticed her shiver, and rubbed her arms and back to induce circulation, but the touch of his capable hands warmed her in entirely different places than those intended. With a thank you touch of her lips to his, they settled in a booth by the window.

The main salon and galley displayed an abundance of hot and cold breakfast dishes, and the smell of coffee and freshly baked bread permeated the area. Alex had never been particularly at ease aboard ship, and her view of a rising and falling horizon accompanied by the motion of an exceedingly choppy harbor, proved to be gastro-intestinally challenging for the unaccustomed sailor.

Vera Cruz however, appeared as comfortable with sailing as flying and returned from the galley with a full breakfast. He pushed black coffee in Alex's direction. "You really should sip the coffee."

"Can't. Feel sick."

"Eat something; it will settle your stomach."

"And you come by this knowledge how?"

"Experience."

"Right . . . hellooo, you pilot, not sailor."

"As you well know, I am an accomplished multi-tasker."

"Humor not funny, mister."

"Captain."

"Are you making fun of me?"

He gestured with his thumb and finger. "Little bit."

"Well, you can be as funny as you like when I throw up all over you." She was dealing with an agony of gastric volcanoes. "And what's with this bloody headache?"

"Here, sip some coffee."

She took a sip. "Why are we here anyway? Why the hell didn't we take the tunnel?"

"I thought a sea voyage might be romantic."

"Excuse me?"

"Sea voyage, sunrise over the bows, romance?" He did the Groucho Marx eyebrows.

Bilious green and in distress, she managed a smile. However, there was no escaping the sickening roll of the lightly loaded vessel on an undulating Channel swell. Alex put her head on her arms and slumped onto the table willing the ferry to England.

The minutes seemed like hours, until the ferry's captain announced their imminent arrival into Folkestone.

*

Vera Cruz returned to the car as the most anxious minutes of their journey approached, and after thanking her disembodied savior, Alex went topside to watch the docking.

On deck, Alex was surprised how the fresh air quickly dispelled her queasiness and calmed her headache. Looking landward, she filled her lungs with the bracing sea air, and as the ferry altered course to align with the dock, the keen breeze stirred a mist of briny spray onto her skin. She liked the surprise of it in her face, the salty taste of earth's life-blood on her lips. Closing her eyes, she leaned over the rail to catch more from whitecaps streaming along the hull.

In no time, the ferry's engines slowed forward motion, and the sea-washed smell of kelp wafted atop the churning waves. Before her, the shining specter of the old Folkestone church loomed large, and a welcoming committee of screeching gulls dipped and dived to the water's brink. She couldn't imagine how sailors managed a voyage lasting months, but she did understand their relief and not inconsiderable joy at pulling safely into port. She knew she'd never appreciate the lure of the sea, but was sure, should she sail again, it would be in an open boat, with the wind in her face.

The shrill wailing of the ferry's siren broke into her daydream. A voice requested passengers return to their cars for offloading, and the minute she ventured below, her nausea returned. Fortunately, her sojourn in the belly of the beast was short-lived, and the ferry barely thumped into its berth before stevedores were directing vehicles onto the dock. Opening her window for a breath of air, Alex celebrated their return to terra firma.

*

Vera Cruz shrunk into stony silence.

Folkestone's formalities were more thorough than Calais. Immigration asked the purpose and duration of Vera Cruz's visit, and for a second time copied his passport. Then customs officers performed a mechanical sweep of the vehicle inside and out, and told Vera Cruz to wait. For several agonizing seconds, his fingers drummed the steering wheel, and just as he thought he might be in trouble, an officer waved the Spider on. Having made the crossing several times, it seemed to Vera Cruz that the officers were more animated than usual. Nevertheless, eager to be on his way while his luck was holding, he pushed the why and wherefore to the back of his mind.

*

From the terminus, Vera Cruz headed toward Radnor Park taking twenty minutes to negotiate the city's convoluted one-way system. They arrived at The Garden Hotel, opposite Central railway station, and he parked in the hotel's rear lot.

Once inside, the front desk clerk, a large, jolly gentleman called Leon, greeted Vera Cruz with warmth and seeming familiarity. And as he filled out a registration card, Leon cheerfully imparted his knowledge of all things Folkestone, heavily endorsing a local restaurant called Serendipity. There, he gushed, "one could enjoy an intimate dinner in the Mediterranean style, and should they desire, he would make them a reservation."

Alex felt sure Vera Cruz would have the clerk book a table, but surprisingly, he declined. She said nothing and, accepting whatever her lover had in mind, followed the bellhop upstairs.

In their suite, Alex wasn't entirely surprised to find a table set with lunch for two and a stand containing iced champagne. Once again, she wondered how Vera Cruz managed to pre-arrange these little affairs in every place they stayed, but when she turned to ask what magic powers he had, he wasn't there. Brushing past the bellhop, she went out to the corridor; he was nowhere to be seen. "Didn't Captain Vera Cruz follow us?" she asked.

"Don't think so, ma'am, maybe he had a job for Leon."

"Yes, I'm sure that's it. He probably wants to know about trains for tomorrow."

"Trains, ma'am?"

"Yes, we need to book my trip north and his to London."

"There's a ticket here, I got it yesterday." He handed Alex a British Rail ticket from the dresser.

"Thank you. That was very kind."

"All part of our Premier Club service, ma'am."

"What's that?"

"One of the perks for our regular guests."

"And what is construed as regular?"

"Not entirely sure of the rules, ma'am, but I think you have to stay at least once a month."

"Well, thank you. Here . . . " Alex offered him a tip. "This is for you."

"Not necessary, ma'am. There are no gratuities for our Premier guests." He handed Alex the key. "Have a nice stay."

As she watched the young man leave, Alex was confused. How could Vera Cruz be in Folkestone once a month when according to him, his flight rotation only occasionally brought him to the UK? Mysterious and alluring at first, her lack of knowledge about the captain's comings and goings was now beginning to rankle. Once again, she found herself exasperated, with a million unanswered questions, waiting for him to appear from who knows where.

As she looked from the window, neither the serenity of Radnor Park nor the ocean view placated her. Moreover, when a movement below caught her eye, and she saw the Spider leaving the hotel's parking lot, her anger swelled. She had her ticket home, so was he simply leaving her in Folkestone? Would she get one of those "sorry I had to leave you" phone calls she so hated? Then she remembered the whole purpose of their trip was to deliver the car to Vera Cruz's friend. Chastising herself for being overly dramatic, she realized her lover had probably waited in the lobby for his friend to pick up the car. But why hadn't he simply told her that? Why was she never privy, in advance, to a single thing in his life?

Alex had been alone for twenty-five minutes when she heard

a key-card in the door. She was no longer angry, just determined to address her concerns with Vera Cruz. But he did not enter. All she saw was a hand around the door holding a single white rose, waving it as if a flag of surrender, and she couldn't help smiling. Stepping forward, she attempted to take the flower. He held it fast, and before she could protest, Vera Cruz was inside, arms around her waist, mouth locked on hers.

This was what Alex both loved and hated about him—his spontaneity. She found it intoxicating and confusing and sexy and irritating. But when he kissed her with passion she'd never felt with anyone else, all was forgiven.

"I hate it when you disappear like that. Where were you?"

"Waiting for my friend to pick up the car."

"Couldn't you have told me that? Introduced me maybe?"

"Didn't think you'd approve."

"Approve? Why not, would I find another woman?"

"See, there you go, jumping to conclusions."

"So why didn't you say anything?"

"Didn't think it was important. Besides I was gone ten minutes, you can't do without me for ten minutes?"

"It was twenty-five, and no I can't. I only get to see you once in a blue moon, and every minute is precious."

"I don't get here that often, you know that."

"Do I?"

"Come on, Alex, we've had this conversation." He grinned. "So, if time is so precious, why are we wasting it talking?"

"Got something else on your mind?"

He began to unbutton her blouse. "Strip, woman—I have work to do."

CHAPTER TWENTY-THREE

December third arrived ominously, with an overcast sky and rain not far off. As she and Vera Cruz silently waited for the train that would take her away from him, Alex's mood was as gloomy as the Folkestone morning. The last few months with her mysterious lover had been a whirlwind journey leaving her body addicted and her mind enslaved. And now, despite surrendering to his will and allowing him to consume her reason, she still had no idea how he felt about her. She'd repeatedly told him she loved him, even pledged her undying devotion, but he'd been surprisingly unaffected by her admissions. She'd tried to find out why he popped in and out of her life without warning or explanation, but despite her best efforts, he'd masterfully averted her questions. As the rain beat down on the platform's roof, she willed him to say something, anything, that would make her feel there was commitment from him. But he did not.

As Alex unconsciously dropped her head to his shoulder, she sensed a familiar soul destroying distance. And a deep insecurity she thought under control returned. Now, just minutes before the train's arrival, she looked deep inside. Deep enough to realize that sporadic moments of unadulterated bliss might be all she would ever get from him. And she was suddenly unsure whether she could live that way. She could, she told herself, because when they were together, he took her to seven kinds of heaven.

But wasn't it usual for lovers to share where they were going, and what they were doing? Wasn't it normal to want to know if your lover actually cared about you? Wasn't it okay to want to know that the relationship was important? But if she pressed him, would she jeopardize the little they had? And, being realistic, what exactly was it they had? Hating herself for being weak and needing him so desperately, Alex had to face facts—he'd been up front from the beginning, and she had no basis to force their relationship to a place he didn't want it to go. Was she simply afraid he wouldn't come back? She'd spent her life pitying dependent women who lived and breathed only to pander to the whims of the man in their life. But, like them, she was now condoning Vera Cruz's emotional darkness, because she was terrified of being alone. And as Alex's mind drifted to a world without him, a tear slid down her cheek.

*

Vera Cruz felt her grip tighten on his arm, and recognized it as a cry for possession. He lifted her head and kissed her tenderly. And though he was a master at his despicable craft, even he was surprised how easily he'd won this particular game. Like all successful couriers he constantly looked for ways to change his patterns in case he was being watched. And considering how uneventfully he had negotiated customs in both France and England, having Alex along on the trip had been a sound decision. Moreover, he not only had her committed to him, but as she became more deeply entrenched in his operation, he knew he could persuade her to do anything.

*

At precisely 9:26 a.m. on the loneliest and most desolate of anyone's December mornings, Alex watched the northbound train clatter onto the platform. There were few passengers and while the bitter cold had them quickly boarding, she hung back clinging to Vera Cruz. She hoped something might change to keep them together, but he simply brushed away her tears and handed her aboard.

As he stepped away from the train, she remained by the door frantically tugging on the strap of the frozen drop window. She badly needed to feel a last embrace and taste his lips on hers. But the whistle sounded, brakes released, and the train lumbered from the station. Alex felt impossibly alone as she continued to pound on the glass. The window stuck fast. Then, as the train chugged beyond the protection of the station buildings, the window released. Leaning out, as far as safety would allow, she scanned the platform. He was gone. And with the train's speed building and the frigid sea air beating against her face, her tears froze.

CHAPTER TWENTY-FOUR

Vera Cruz walked from the station to be met at the curb by a familiar green sports car. Throwing his bags into the trunk, he slid into the passenger seat, reached over, and ran his fingers up the inside of Red's thigh. They exchanged no words; she merely handed him some newspaper clippings and headed for Heathrow.

Vera Cruz smiled as he scanned the clippings from Italian newspapers. They all reported the same incident.

"On his return from a business trip to Paris, Count Victor Centrini reported to local police authorities that a picture, attributed to Luca Giordano, was stolen from his villa in the fashionable northern village of Rovereto. A thief apparently entered the Villa Maggiore, leaving no discernible signs of damage, and authorities are looking into rumors of complicity. The beleaguered Count is known to have been experiencing financial difficulties, brought about by several failed business ventures, and the picture was recently insured by the Musea de Medici group for Euro 1.5 million. A full investigation is ongoing."

*

It was late afternoon when Red left the airport hotel and Vera Cruz could finally concentrate on his delivery schedule. However, upon calling his villa in Portugal, he got the answering machine.

"Pete, I'm at Heathrow for the December fourth pick-up. I'll drop that package in Rome before returning home to Ericeira—"

"Yo," Pete interrupted.

"You're home, what gives, you know I hate leaving messages."

"Sorry, boss, was on the other line. Some Paki I didn't recognize has another delivery—Karachi to London."

"Did he know the password?"

"Yeah, said his name is Rajak. Purdy's nephew. Purdy took sick and he's standing in. That's why it's a rush job."

"Does it come through Franco?"

"No. Off the grid. Money's all yours and they're paying double."

"How heavy?"

"Thirty-five kilos, maybe a little more."

"Shit, I'm not sure. That needs some thought. You know the timing stinks and . . . what do we have outstanding?"

"Just the bag in Abu Dhabi. We got paid for the picture, and the wire transfer for the Spider came through about an hour ago. Look, boss, I know you want to make the bag's microfilm your last delivery, so if you want to call it a day and let this Paki go to hell, I'm with you."

"Yeah, I know, but two hundred thousand is hard to turn down. Is there any way we can squeeze in a quick run while we wait for the bag to be sorted out?"

"We can if the bastards in Karachi don't bleed us dry. You know they're circling like vultures, waiting for us to croak. And this is way close to the last delivery."

"I know. Let's move on 'til I can get my head around this one. Anything else?"

"Yeah, and it might help your head. Got a message from Jim at Heathrow—some dude called Shivazi has your bag in Abu Dhabi's lost and found. Jim got on to him, and it cost plenty, but he's routing it back to Heathrow as crew baggage. It's on an Emirates flight, leaving Abu Dhabi on December tenth. It'll arrive with the Purser, and as Emirates flights are not in Jim's area, a friend at GAP will pick it up from the aircraft and store it in Baggage Facilities until someone picks it up. There's already a baggage search trail in place, so when the bag arrives, it'll be seen as a regular lost bag. You just have to get someone to clear it through customs."

"Don't need to. This could work out perfectly. We do the extra run and we'll already be there."

"Run it by me."

"Thirty-five kilos is pretty heavy, so I'm guessing it'll go in the hold, and be routinely offloaded at Heathrow. Jim can store it out back in the usual spot. When we arrive, I'll stop at the GAP baggage office and remove the microfilm from my flight bag. I'll tell them I have an appointment and will return later. While I deliver the film, you can meander down to crew control, swing out back, pick up the Karachi piece, and carry it out through staff security. Then we'll meet at Red's and wait for the wire transfer before returning home."

"Once you've got the film, are you going to abandon your old flight bag?"

"Can't. Have some stones, passports, a bunch of money, and my gun. I'll pick it up myself and carry it back to Lisbon."

"Why don't you just have GAP re-tag and route it?"

"And lose it again?"

"See what you mean, but it's too risky for you to go back a second time. I'll pick it up and carry it."

"That'll work. Thanks, Pete. The five grand in it is yours."

"You're all heart, boss."

CHAPTER TWENTY-FIVE

Jake had had a bad feeling about the captain from day one. And it wasn't simply because the pilot had made a move on Alex. He'd been following a group of rogue pilots for months, but no matter where an incident occurred, he couldn't isolate them in his sights. Now, with a potential firestorm brewing, he had to convince Alex she might be getting involved in something more than she could handle. Something that, once in, even he couldn't bail her out.

"Alex, it's me," he said, for the third time into her answering machine. "For the record, I want you to know I'm not spying or prying or any other sort of surveillance nonsense. I care about you so much, I don't want you to do anything that might get you into trouble. Having said that, I called passenger and spoke to Sarah. She said you'd taken off across Europe with that pilot. Nobody knows exactly where you are or how long you'll be gone. Sweetie, seriously, what are you thin . . . okay, you're right, your love life is none of my business. Look, I know this sounds melodramatic, but I'm working a potentially dangerous case, and we have to talk face-to-face. I want to explain as best I can what I'm doing, and how you could get hurt. Not emotionally hurt, Alex, although that's probably a given. I mean hurt, hurt, body damaged, blood-spilling hurt. Please call me as soon as you get home. I promise, no lectu—"

Weeeeeee. The machine cut him off.

"Shit," he said, slamming down the phone. "I have got to speak to her about that—"

"Got to speak to who about what?"

"Hi, Eddie, Alex's frigging answer phone keeps cutting me off."

"Still leaving messages? Thought you were going to speak to her about—you know—the two of you."

"I was, but stuff got in the way."

"Pilot stuff?"

"Something like that."

"Jake, seriously, if she's with that guy, you can't tell her anything. You know if she even hints that we're watching him, it could seriously compromise the investigation. If the Super found out, you'd be busted down to beat cop. You have to let her go and whatever happens, so be it."

"Can't, Ed, I care too much about her."

"And does she care anything about you? If she won't even return your calls—"

"She's left messages, plenty of 'em. I was just so pissed off and jealous, I didn't want to talk to her."

"So continue with that; leave her be."

"It's not that easy."

"So let's assume you go in all gangbusters, knight in shining armor. Is she gonna dump the fly boy and be with you?"

"I don't know."

"I do. Face it, bro, she made her choice. Now you have to step back and let it play out."

"I told you, I'm not sure I can do that."

"Well, you better be damn sure she's not involved in anything, because if you're wrong you'll get crucified."

CHAPTER TWENTY-SIX

When the captain approached Gate 22 on December fourth to pick up what he knew was a quantity of undocumented diamonds, he found it occupied by an Al Italia flight. "Hi, Dave," he said to the dispatcher. "I was expecting the Air Porto here, what gives?"

"Sorry, captain, snafu on the ramp. Baggage conveyor hit a sensor and engineering is taking a look at it. We'll be at least forty late so your incoming was re-directed to Stand Thirty."

"That the third spot off the pier?"

"Yeah, it's a ways, you need a ride?"

"No, that's ok. I'll call my crew control."

"Sorry, no can do. Phone's out. I can patch you through on my radio."

Glancing at his watch, Vera Cruz had less than thirty minutes to get over to terminal three for his ride to Karachi, and with no way to contact Jim to confirm whether the package was on the engineer's box below or transferred to Air Porto's new location, he had no choice. "Don't bother, I'll walk. By the time anyone gets here I'll be off my slot too."

"Suit yourself, but keep your eyes on the baggage guys. New intake, they think the ramp's a race track."

Vera Cruz knew he risked exposure if he was seen rooting around the ramp, and it wasn't a risk worth taking. If his package was near the engineer's box, he'd bag it and take the shuttle bus directly to PIA operations. If it wasn't, he'd assume it had been moved to Stand 30, where it could stay until Jim did his follow-up.

Proceeding down the ramp stairs, the pilot saw a familiar manila envelope with a purple stripe partially protruding from the trashcan inside the ramp door. Jim had modified the original pick-up location. The captain smiled. Clearly their last conversation had hit home. Stashing the envelope in his flight bag, he stepped onto the ramp, doubled back to the transit lounge bus stop, and hopped on the shuttle to terminal three.

*

The long haul to Karachi was uneventful with a good deal of down time, so Vera Cruz took the opportunity to cultivate useful colleagues. He never knew when he might need a ride, and on this occasion, he endeared himself to the PIA flight deck. They had several London night-stops in their rotation and were looking for a good hangout. Vera Cruz gave them passes to the most happening club in London—REDS. And, by way of a thank you, the PIA captain suggested Vera Cruz join them on the following week's flight back to London. That unexpected outcome totally suited his plan. Not only would there be no problem having the case he was collecting loaded as deadhead-crew baggage, but more importantly, being listed as crew meant his movements would not be so closely scrutinized by the Pakistani authorities.

CHAPTER TWENTY-SEVEN

Shivazi was disturbed when he received a message from Jim in London. He knew other baggage agents providing his type of service were paid a lot more than he was, and he had never been asked to risk exposure by handling a courier's bag more than once. Now, the urgency to ship this one afforded him the opportunity to demand triple dollars for its transfer.

It was easy to create a false shipping record. And while everybody in baggage handling knew that Abu Dhabi's customs officers were conducting magnifying glass checks on anything going to London, with legitimate clearance documents, he could simply take it to the aircraft and have it loaded as a secure crew bag.

At the aircraft, Shivazi was directed to the flight deck for approval to carry, and the baggage handler's performance in the cockpit was masterful. Sharing a story about a fellow pilot, anxiously waiting his misrouted property, the first officer checked tags, clearances, and seals, and the bag was accepted for carriage.

Near bursting with excitement, Shivazi swaggered back to the baggage office. He could hardly wait to tell his supervisor that he quit. However, as he entered the arrival's hall, he found customs officials going through the baggage lock up. No one ever knew when their spot check might uncover some type of illicit material, but he wasn't worried—the one bag that would change his life had escaped their scrutiny.

Confident as a newly wealthy baggage handler can be, Shivazi entered lost and found and calmly closed the flight bag's file in the computer. Within an instant, a message hit GAP at Heathrow advising them the bag was on the flight. And when the auto acknowledgement bounced back, Shivazi opened a box of archive documents and buried the file. He had no doubt that whatever happened at Heathrow, he would be long gone before anything traced back to him.

The young opportunist floated on air as he thought of his girlfriend. Finally he had more to impress her family than a baggage handler's salary. And as he approached her, there was no mistaking the look of achievement on his face.

*

At the same moment Shivazi was whispering his intentions in his girlfriend's ear, his supervisor was removing a file from the archive box. And he handed that file to a waiting official.

CHAPTER TWENTY-EIGHT

Europa's ticket desk had worked miracles rebooking and rerouting passengers with missed connections. Now only the arrival of the returning aircraft with its missed land connections was left. In no rush to return to an empty house, Alex volunteered to stay late and deal with those.

As Alex waited on the pier, she would have liked to clear the hectic day from her head, but the night was too cold and damp to venture onto the ramp. The solitude of the empty building gave her the quiet time she needed to think about recent events. And deny as she might, she couldn't shake the notion that since she met Vera Cruz, an insidious dissatisfaction had overtaken her life. It was as if he'd consumed her spirit, bringing out a needy, desperate somebody else.

For a million different reasons, many of which made no sense, she loved and hated him. She craved his body as much as the power he wielded over her repulsed her. She ached for his touch in the midst of being afraid of the exquisite pain he inflicted. She had never been so confused, and her only certainty was that whichever way she looked at herself, with or without Vera Cruz, her priorities had shifted. The self-sufficient life she'd come to terms with, and for the most part enjoyed, no longer fit. And there was absolutely nothing she could do about it. Jake had been the only person who understood her enough to talk her through such things, and they'd been playing phone tag for what seemed like an eternity.

As Alex fought to resolve her misgivings, the flight arrived. Fortunately, there were only seven displaced passengers, all easy to deal with, so as December tenth came to a close, Alex signed off and headed uphill to the staff parking area. Every time she walked it now, she expected Vera Cruz to appear from nowhere. Tonight, he did not.

Wrapping her scarf tighter about her neck, she couldn't shake the chill that had lately lodged in her bones. And her mind was in turmoil. *I'm still young, I could travel, find myself a steady guy. Why am I continuing to put up with days like today? And why am I holding a bloody candle for someone who doesn't give a shit about my feelings?*

She drove home on autopilot, her mind filled with thoughts of what she might do to be with Vera Cruz. And she almost convinced herself to quit her job to be available to him when and wherever he wanted. But her mind wouldn't settle.

Alex entered her house by the front door and emptied the letterbox hoping he might have sent her a card. There was only junk mail, and throwing it on the hallstand, she caught a glimpse of herself in the mirror. Her appearance shocked her. It was now obvious that long shifts and worrying about where Vera Cruz might be were taking a toll on her health. She looked more than tired, had lost weight, and the darkening shadow across her eyes clearly indicated her emotions were shredded. She'd felt similarly after her husband died—the smallest provocation reduced her to tears. Now, as she stared back at this ragged person, the distress of loss was evident on her face.

Swiping a hand across her eyes didn't stop the tears. Her husband had been one thing, but she never imagined a man who'd given so shallowly of himself could reduce her to such a vulnerable state. She walked through the empty house knowing only Vera Cruz's presence could pull her out of the funk into which she'd fallen.

Throwing her coat and bag onto the sofa, Alex kicked off her shoes, went to the fridge, and poured a large glass of wine. She quickly dispatched it hoping it would calm her enough to get some of the sleep that had been eluding her for the past few days. It did not. So she took another. With a second glass by her side, she recalled what had happened in Folkestone and at the train station, and tried to work out why he hadn't contacted her. She could think of nothing and finally persuaded herself that something dire had happened to him. And as she drained the second glass without benefit of food, the wine achieved what she wanted. Her body relaxed, her mind dulled enough to calm her anxiety, and she drifted into the desperate unconsciousness brought on by alcohol.

*

When the phone startled her awake, she snatched up the handset, expecting to hear Vera Cruz. A woman spoke. She sounded old.

"Hello, Mrs.," she said with a heavy accent. "You don't knowing me, and I calling to you about man who is not who you think."

"What are you saying, I can barely hear you." The caller seemed light years away. "Who is this?"

"He was engaging my daughter, and I am taking your number from in her house after she has dying." The voice broke into sobs, and the line went dead.

Not knowing what to make of it, Alex put down the handset and sunk back into alcohol-induced sleep. The phone woke her again. Rubbing her neck from sleeping awkwardly, Alex looked at her watch. It was 2:30 a.m. She lifted the receiver for the second time, and another heavily accented voice spoke. This time, a younger man.

"Hello, miss, please forgive my intrusion, but I am compelled to call and warn you of great danger."

"Who the hell is this?" she snapped. "What do you want?"

"Apologies, miss, my name is Tariq Mohammed, and I am calling from Karachi in Pakistan. My sister-in-law Maleka Miranabar worked as a flight attendant for Pakistan International

Airlines and was befriended by a Captain Velasquez, who is your friend also, I think?"

"I don't know any—"

"Please, miss, it is important you believe me. This captain asked Maleka to take a package to Lisbon. When she returned to Karachi someone in crew reporting told her the police were looking for her. They said she had delivered drugs, and was going to be arrested. Rather than bring shame on our family, she drove into a friend's garage, locked the door, and sat with the engine running. She killed herself."

"My God, I am so sorry but—"

"We are also sorry. We knew nothing of her relationship with this man until it was too late. But it is not too late for you. We are thinking he will make you do bad things too. Please, Miss Alex, your name and number were on a paper in Maleka's house, and I have to warn you before he hurts you."

Alex listened, barely comprehending. "Mr. Mohammed I don't know anyone called Velasquez, and I certainly wouldn't be stupid enough to take drugs anywhere, for anybody. I'm sorry for your loss, and I don't mean to be rude, but you're mistaken, I'm not the person you need to talk to."

Before the caller could continue, Alex severed the connection. But as she thought about the strange voice in the night, she was jolted awake. How would someone in Pakistan just run across her phone number? And what were the odds of two women on opposite sides of world being acquainted with a captain who asked them to deliver a parcel? For weeks he'd turned up out-of-the-blue, having spent time God knows where. He never answered questions about his personal life; she didn't even know here he lived. And God knew he made her do things she'd never even thought about, let alone done with any man before. But a drug dealer? Unlikely. Crews are too closely scrutinized by customs and bound by FAA regulations and airline procedures. Besides, she would know if he were a criminal. She was smart enough to recognize the signs.

Then images of an envelope and a picture from Rome popped into her head. Did they count? Was giving him back his own property and delivering something to a friend illegal? No, they were nothing. Mr. Mohammed was wrong. It was a case of mistaken identity. She pushed the whole business to the back of her mind, and fell asleep.

*

About the time Alex was drifting into sleep, the night shift sergeant of Heathrow's Special Branch received the message he'd been told to look out for.

The flight bag that had dropped off the radar several weeks previously had been located in Abu Dhabi. Moreover, it was being shipped back to London as crew baggage on Emirates 079, landing on December eleventh at 8.30 a.m.

The officer logged in the message and acknowledged its receipt to his colleagues in the United Arab Emirates. Then, tearing off the print out, he put a large red arrow next to the text and taped it to Jake Fowler's monitor.

CHAPTER TWENTY-NINE

When the cabin door of Emirates flight 079 swung open, the GAP baggage agent was waiting. Taking bag and paperwork from the purser, he walked casually back to the arrival's hall, re-tagged the bag, and logged it in the computer using the dummy file created several days previously. Then he placed it in the customs lock-up. Knowing it would remain untouched unless customs did a spot check or someone picked it up, he walked to a pay phone and left Jim a message.

*

Victoria Tate, an undercover police officer, had been floating through various airlines passenger departments for some weeks and had monitored the baggage handler's movements since he took the bag from the Emirates purser. She watched as he made his phone call and radioed Jake. She confirmed the baggage office closed for lunch at twelve-thirty, at which time he could conduct his search.

*

Jake drove from the central police station through Heathrow's tunnel to terminal three, and arriving at the Special Branch office, he reviewed the updated case file, noting that the investigation had started in Antwerp, when four pilots began selling large quantities of unregistered diamonds smuggled out of South Africa. The investigation emphasis changed to terrorism, and Special Branch had become involved when an informant told Antwerp police that some diamonds, converted to cash, had paid for a pilot's flight bag to be secreted at London's Heathrow airport. That bag supposedly contained a microfilm with instructions for a terrorist attack on dams and bridges in the United States.

At first, Special Branch had doubts about the reliability of the Belgian data, understanding that informants, though a necessary evil, often gave bogus information to make easy money. However, as they were closing in to search the bag, it disappeared.

That had been some weeks previous, and since then, Jake had connected enough dots to believe the bag did hold plans for some kind of terrorist assault and that whoever was protecting the bag at Heathrow had routed it to the Middle East to avoid scrutiny. Now he was as close as he'd ever been to tying UK staff, the rogue pilots on his watch-list, and the contents of the flight bag together. He wouldn't lose it again.

After contacting the customs watch commander, Jake was assigned a search specialist, and the men entered the baggage hall. Using a building master key, they accessed the GAP office and quickly located the flight bag. It was hauled onto a table, where customs opened it with a universal key and combination tumbler and the men methodically reviewed the contents. They found flight manuals, several blank airline tickets, a shaving foam dispenser hiding several thousand American dollars, and correspondence indicating the bag's owner was involved in relationships with several women. And Jake had no choice but to readjust his thinking. Whatever he was looking for wasn't as obvious as he thought. But there must be something in the bag to make its owner want it so badly.

As Jake studied each item, he wracked his brain to tie something to his investigation. From experience, he knew that unendorsed tickets might be suspicious for the general public. But airline personnel often carry them to accommodate spontaneous changes in travel plans. And while the money was substantial, it wasn't unreasonable for a frequent traveler in today's economy. However, upon closer scrutiny the correspondence set off alarms in his head. And as he picked through the letters, he isolated an unopened envelope addressed to a Captain Velasquez at PIA in Lisbon, found an open one addressed to Captain Girgenti in Rome, and a note-card for a Captain Duchevne in Paris. Three of the four names on his rogue pilot's watch-list. Only Vera Cruz was absent.

Jake smiled. It wasn't a stretch to conclude that the four pilots wanted by the authorities were the same person.

*

With their search completed, and nothing resembling a film found, the customs specialist re-locked the flight bag. Then, tagging it Day-Glo orange—"cleared waiting claimant,"—he repositioned it with others in the lock-up.

Jake knew that when such bags are claimed, they must be taken through customs' "something to declare," and there the clearing officer's computer throws up a file corresponding with the bag tag number. The usual purpose is to collect any duty before closing it in the system, but this bag was also assigned a computerized red flag, identifying it as needing detailed information on the claimant.

Before leaving customs, Jake organized a tap on outgoing calls from the arrival hall. And he requested comprehensive background checks of GAP baggage staff and airline personnel to see if any had connections to each other, or the Middle East.

*

When the GAP agent returned from lunch, he noticed the bags he so carefully positioned had been re-arranged. However, his nerves calmed when he saw all the bags had orange tags. Customs had simply made a spot check and cleared them. Mentally patting himself on the back for putting one over on the authorities, he used a pay phone to advise Jim his bag was ready for pick up.

CHAPTER THIRTY

For weeks, Vera Cruz had spontaneously appeared at the airport or on Alex's doorstep. Now, it seemed like forever since she'd seen or heard from him. She enquired about him through PIA's crew-control, but they made it clear policy forbade them from giving out personal information about their pilots. She asked cabin crew colleagues who flew his routes if they had seen him on layovers. But no one seemed to have any more idea about his whereabouts than she did. Then, during a moment of clarity, she swallowed her pride and called Jake for help.

"Where have you been?" he said. "I've been leaving messages like a lunatic."

"You could have talked to me at work, I've been back a while."

"I've been off site a lot."

"You, off site? Where?"

"Scotland Yard first, then Federale Politie in Antwerp, Interpol in Paris, stuff like that."

"I was in Europe too."

"I heard. So what gives? I guess it's the captain Eddie saw you with?"

"It is."

"Look Alex, I'm not comfortable with you—"

"Excuse me?"

"Sorry. I'll put that another way. I have reason to believe—"

"Oh, for God's sake. Are you going to get all Sherlock Holmes on me about Tayo?"

"Tayo?"

"Tayo Vera Cruz, that's his name."

"Oh, Jesus."

"Uh?"

"Alex, please, I'm not being deliberately obtuse, but I just can't say too much. I can only ask that you stop seeing this guy."

"We went through all this before. I thought we agr—"

"I'm not talking about me being jealous, this is about you. It's about protecting you because I care for you."

"You want me to dump a man I'm crazy about because you 'care' for me?"

"You know it's more than that."

"Do I?"

"Christ, you know it is. I love you, Alex. I've always loved you. How could you not see that?"

"Because you're always Mr. Hot-Shot Special Branch, cool and detached from the world. You didn't show it, and you never said a word. What am I, psychic?"

"No, and again, I'm sorry. You're absolutely right."

"So why didn't you say something sooner?"

"I was trying to be respectful after your husband died. Then you got involved with other people and I didn't want to come over all jealous and bitter."

"But you did, right when I met Tayo."

"He's different. I can't say any more, Alex. Please trust me— you have to stop seeing him."

"Just like that, because you say so."

"Why do you always twist everything so I sound like a jerk?"

"So give me a reason. One solid reason . . . apart from you not liking him."

"I can't. I just can't."

"Then I believe this conversation is over." She slammed down the phone.

Alex was disappointed with Jake. She'd thought they had squared away their differences over Vera Cruz. But more than being disappointed, she'd never heard him so dogmatic about something without giving her his reasoning. He was straightforward about everything, that's why she so valued his opinion. Now, while she knew he might have her best interests in mind, his tone was irritatingly evasive. And she didn't like it.

As the minutes ticked by, Alex really expected Jake to call her back. And when he didn't, she couldn't imagine what she'd done to alienate him so that he'd gotten to the point of being officious. They'd spent so much time together after her husband and his fiancée died. He was the one person who understood her pain, and what it was like to be desperately lonely. He was a kindred spirit who walked her through her relationship mistakes, knowing she was simply trying to recapture the feeling of belonging. He was the one someone who alleviated her doubts and fears, and convinced her that in the end, everything would turn out right. Now, in losing her dearest friend's counsel, she had no one but herself to rely on.

CHAPTER THIRTY-ONE

Karachi airport was abuzz with activity, and as Vera Cruz made his way through the terminal crush to PIA's offices, he saw Pete in line at the first-class desk. His almost imperceptible nod confirmed things were going as planned, and once clear of the check-in area, Vera Cruz moved quickly to the relative calm of PIA operations.

Captain Akbar had arranged his ride back to the UK and was waiting for him in the ready room. And as the pilots greeted each other, Vera Cruz learned they would be making a technical stop in Rome. He was delighted. The aircraft would be on the ground for an hour to offload engine parts for a stranded PIA aircraft, so he could call his airport contact to relieve him of Franco's diamonds.

*

Flight PK 126 from Karachi to London was ready to depart. Captain Akbar had signed off final documents indicating the aircraft contained the correct number of passengers, bags, freight, and operating crew, plus a deadheading captain occupying a jump seat. And while both captains were anxious, for entirely different reasons, as pushback neared, engineering radioed that it would take a few more minutes to load the engine parts. Vera Cruz had been through similar delays a thousand times, but that did nothing to quell his uneasiness. Moreover, with minutes left, he'd not seen his PIA contact, and the bag he came to Karachi for had not yet arrived.

As the flight deck received word they'd closed the final hold, Vera Cruz glanced at his watch. It appeared the supposedly urgent shipment, which had put him at considerable risk to accompany, would not make the flight. And though questions would surely arise when he arrived in London, it was not his problem. He quietly accepted he'd made a wasted journey, until he heard a commotion behind him.

Looking back, Vera Cruz could see a breathless baggage handler, lugging a large black case into the galley area. He told the dispatcher it was an additional aircraft part, destined for Heathrow, and that load control had neglected to put it on the manifest.

The dispatcher presented Captain Akbar with more papers, the first officer went back to check the tags and seals, and it was accepted as bulk-load cargo in hold five.

From where he was sitting, Vera Cruz watched the proceedings, and while he hadn't recognized the baggage handler, he was very familiar with the purple stripe marking the side of the large industrial case. He quietly breathed a sigh of relief; a substantial bonus was riding on that case.

*

A bright winter morning greeted PIA's arrival in Rome. However, an unusually heavy volume of vehicles buzzed around the terminal stands. Rolling along, Captain Akbar didn't seem bothered by the fully occupied terminal gates, as he was simply dropping off aircraft parts. But as they trundled toward a remote stand, it was clear to Vera Cruz that he must abandon his plan to have someone collect Franco's diamonds.

The pilots looked side to side and around their aircraft, but as they pulled into place, Vera Cruz was concerned by the unusual police presence around the stand to which they'd been directed. And as the aircraft rocked to a stop, he asked Captain Akbar if he'd ever experienced this amount of ground traffic without some sort of emergency being declared. The operating captain replied in the negative, and radioed the tower for clarification. He was told his flight was subject to a random security screening relating to the aircraft parts he was transporting. Neither Akbar nor Vera Cruz bought the explanation as everything had been cleared in Karachi before they left; nevertheless, they sat back accepting that spot checks had become an annoying, but necessary, part of airline travel.

As was usual with an aircraft on the ground, the purser opened the forward cabin door. And to facilitate boarding of an airport authority representative, airport handling pushed steps toward the aircraft. However, once the equipment was in position, a man and an armed police officer mounted it. As they made the steep climb upward and came through the cabin toward the cockpit, the hackles on Vera Cruz's neck bristled. He knew they were coming for him.

Apologizing for the intrusion, the man requested a moment with Captain Vera Cruz and in broken English told him there had been a catastrophic accident within his family. They were escorting him to another carrier for an immediate flight home.

After collecting his bags from the crew locker, the pilot was seated in the waiting police car. There, with Zen-like resignation, he watched as the case with the purple stripe was removed from the cargo hold.

*

The drive to Fiumicino airport's police headquarters took a few minutes and Vera Cruz was neither handcuffed nor treated like a suspect. That was a good sign, but as this was not his first brush with the European authorities, the captain knew how to play the game.

At the police station, Vera Cruz was shown to a brightly lit room containing easy chairs, a table strewn with magazines and newspapers, a coffee machine, a water cooler, and a phone. He'd bypassed any sort of booking desk, wasn't in a holding cell, and was invited to make himself comfortable. He decided not to tip his hand by speaking Italian, and in English asked the police escort what was going on. The officer shrugged and indicated they were waiting for a translator.

Vera Cruz inwardly smiled. Clearly, the airport police weren't sure what they were dealing with, and didn't have anyone with sufficient English to attempt an interrogation. Maintaining a deferential attitude, Vera Cruz gestured to the policeman that he needed to use the phone. The officer nodded in agreement and left.

Dialing a local number, the familiar lisp of his agent came on the phone.

"Pronto, Franco Di Roselli—"

"This is Tayo."

"Um, I am surprised to hear from you. You have news for me?"

"Franco, dear uncle, forgive my intrusion at so early an hour, but it seems an anniversary gift I have for Aunt Aida might be too big for me to carry alone."

Though his bulk made him sluggish, Franco wasn't a stupid man. Vera Cruz knew he would immediately associate his use of buzzwords with his carrying a shipment. "How so, nephew, it is but a small token of my affection, much like the gifts of past years."

"I thought something a little larger and more exotic might sit well with her, so I made a special trip. Now I have been invited to speak to the Italian authorities, but I hope to, very soon, see you both."

"But nephew," Franco cooed into the phone, "I was not expecting this. She is here at the villa—how did you plan on hiding this gift?"

"Maybe with someone else in the family. She will never know you are involved."

"Good, your discretion calms me and when we meet, I will take account of that. There has undoubtedly been a misunderstanding with the authorities. I will speak to cousin Edmondo within the hour."

In no small way relieved that the wheels to secure his freedom were in motion, Vera Cruz poured a cup of coffee and sat back to wait.

*

It was well into the afternoon before the linguistically challenged officer returned with an attractive young woman, who introduced herself as the translator. Vera Cruz rose from his chair, and smiling sincerely, offered his hand. She firmly shook it, returned his smile, and gestured for him to sit.

"Captain Vera Cruz," she began, "we apologize for bringing you here without explanation, and keeping you waiting so long. Despite being an airport police authority, our bilingual staff resources are limited. And between you and me, with budget cuts everywhere, there is very little chance of the situation improving any time soon."

"I understand, Miss—er, translator. However, I hope you will impress upon the authorities that I am on my way to a very important aviation meeting and if I don't arrive on time, there will be serious international ramifications."

"Yes, captain. I understand the gravity of 'international ramifications.' Nevertheless, the Italian authorities received word from Karachi that a case marked with a purple stripe, containing a substantial quantity of drugs, was on board the aircraft on which you were the captain—"

"I was the captain?"

"Yes, sir, and as such we must investigate the matter. In addition, certain of your personal belongings have been confiscated and are prompting questions."

"Questions that you will now ask?"

"Not at the moment. We are confirming the validity of certain things, which will take time. In the interim, you will remain here."

"Am I a prisoner?"

"No, sir, you are simply helping us with our enquiries."

"Am I to be charged with anything?"

"Not at the moment. You are simply helping us with our enquiries."

"So I can leave and come back later?"

"No, sir, not while you are helping us with our enquiries."

"Can I make phone calls, tell people where I am?"

"Not while—"

"I know, I'm helping you with your enquiries."

"Correct."

"So why exactly are you here?"

"Italian law requires that you understand why you are here."

He raised an eyebrow. "But I don't understand why I'm here."

"We are investigating a very serious accusation which involves you."

The captain knew whatever he said at this point may prove awkward for him in the future, so he used an approach that had proved successful in the past. Looking directly at the translator, he smiled. "Whatever I am accused of, I am totally innocent. Look at my eyes, they are sincere."

She blushed at the intimacy his eyes conveyed.

"You said the accusation of shipping drugs was leveled at the flight's captain?"

"Yes, sir."

"I wasn't the captain on that flight. I was merely hitching a ride to my meeting."

A tiny twitch in the translator's smile conveyed her support for the charismatic pilot. She paused to translate for the policeman, who demanded the captain tell him about the case in the cargo hold. Vera Cruz remained blank until he received a translation.

"I'm not sure what the policeman means," he answered. "My only bags were those stowed in the crew locker inside the aircraft's cabin. The bag you speak of, I presume the one removed from the flight with me, arrived at the last minute. It's not mine. I have no idea from where it came, or to whom it belongs. Moreover, the responsibility for accepting its shipment was not mine. It was the operating captain."

As the translation flowed, a second policeman appeared at the door and whispered to his colleagues.

"Captain Vera Cruz," the translator continued, "it appears communication between Italy and the correct authority in Pakistan is difficult. Sadly, you will have to remain here overnight. Is there someone in London we can contact to alert them of your situation?"

"No, I'll deal with whatever comes."

"Then for now there are no further questions. Thank you for your cooperation, the officer and I will return as soon as more information becomes available."

*

At five-thirty in the afternoon, Franco's lawyer arrived. The short, rotund, balding man, in designer suit and expensive shoes, curtly introduced himself. "You are a lucky man, Captain Vera Cruz. Many people in high places have vouched for your bona fides. And while the police will hold your passport and flight bag pending further investigation, I have secured your conditional release to the villa of Signor Franco Di Roselli. You will be under house arrest until further notice."

"Thank you. Do we go now?"

"Naturally, you will follow me."

*

The drive to Franco's "Villa Varese" was familiar to Vera Cruz. Passing through the heart of Rome and leaving by way of Via Porta Pinciana, the limo crossed the Via Veneto and headed out beyond the Villa Borghese. Then, as they pulled up in front of a sprawling three-story terracotta building, an enormous pair of carriage doors swung open, allowing the vehicle to access an inner courtyard.

When the limo stopped, a steward stepped forward and opened the passenger door. A second removed Vera Cruz's suitcase from the trunk. Then, as the lawyer departed, the trio walked silently into a cavernous entrance hall.

Vera Cruz was shown to an elegantly appointed drawing room, full of antiques, and object d'art. The steward told him he was the villa's only guest, but before he had time to ask questions, a manservant emerged from a concealed panel in a wall of books.

"Good afternoon, Captain Vera Cruz," he said in clipped English. "My master will be calling shortly, and invites you to make yourself at home. Dinner will be served in fifteen minutes, and I took the liberty of chilling a bottle of Cristal . . . unless you would prefer something else?"

"No, Cristal is perfect, and should I need something what do I call you?"

"I am Jeeves, Signor Di Roselli's personal manservant, sir. But you can summon any one of a number of staff by using the fireplace pull."

Vera Cruz smiled. "Jeeves is your real name?"

"No, sir, a little eccentricity on the master's part."

"Well, thank you, Jeeves; I'll be fine." With that, Jeeves bowed respectfully and withdrew from the room.

*

As the hours dragged by Vera Cruz became restless. He'd never been good in any type of captivity, and he needed air. Opening the wall-to-ceiling doors that let out onto a courtyard, he strolled about reflecting on how he might extricate himself from his situation. He came to a stop beside an ornamental pool filled with the same type of koi he had at his home in Ericeira. And as he watched the jewel-hued fish swim gracefully about the reeds and lilies, a calm resignation overtook him. He smiled, knowing there were far worse places to be imprisoned.

*

It was very late when Franco finally called. "What in God's name were you thinking calling my personal line? And since when do you make Karachi runs so close together?" He gave the captain no opportunity to answer. "Have you any idea how much your little escapade has cost me, and how our association might compromise my position?"

The captain knew they were both in danger of losing a great deal, and was in no mood for his agent's hysterics. "I knew the run was risky from the start, but it came through your channels." He lied easily. "I thought I was doing a favor to save your goddamn ass. I was obviously wrong. But I'm not wrong about one of your Karachi people tipping off the authorities. I recognized the handler who brought the bag to the aircraft. He was the talker. Now get the fuck organized, I want out of Italy."

"Don't you presume to—"

"Enough pontificating, Franco. As we sit here, debating the whys and wherefores, the microfilm, which is so important to both our futures, is back at Heathrow. The longer it sits there, the more chance there is of somebody finding it and blowing the whole deal. Think about that for a while, Mr. What The Hell Were You Thinking, because I for one am not about to give up a million dollars because your position might be compromised.

"I dropped everything to do this run for you, now you owe me. Anybody can get the bag out of Heathrow, but you know I'm the only person who can hand over that film, so quit talking about compromising positions. If I go down, believe me you will be close behind. Now tell your fat bastard of a lawyer to get me out of here so I can get back to the UK and deliver that goddamn film."

"Tayo, dear friend, I understand your . . . er . . . our, dilemma, but you must be patient." Franco was uncharacteristically humbled. "I have important friends in the justice office who owe me favors, but eliciting their cooperation will take time—"

"Time is one thing we're short of. Talk to your lawyer, he looks the type to come up with something creative."

"Maybe, but we cannot jeopardize our operation here."

"Screw your operation. If I don't deliver that film, there'll be no operation because we'll both be dead."

"Yes, yes, I understand, but at least I arranged for you to stay at my beautiful villa. Isn't that preferable to jail?"

A derogatory grunt emanated from Vera Cruz.

"Italy has its own way of doing things, dear Tayo, each in its appointed time. You will be at my home for a while; even my 'fat bastard of a lawyer' will find it impossible to change that. Now please relax and let the pieces fall into place."

*

A somber day followed as Vera Cruz considered his options. House arrest wasn't particularly bothersome in such a place. However, his real imprisonment was that in the absence of passports, tickets, or money, should he flee Rome, there was no way he could get out of Italy. This was the first time he'd felt truly trapped, but he knew his saving grace would be Pete. Once he got to London and saw his boss wasn't there, he'd make some calls and find out what happened. Then, knowing Pete, he'd make his way back to Ericeira to await instructions. Vera Cruz would hold off for three days before contacting his colleague.

*

The hours passed slowly until Franco's lawyer re-visited. "Captain Vera Cruz," he began. "I have successfully argued your case. The police admit they haven't enough evidence to charge you with drug smuggling. However, you are being cited for possession of stolen airline tickets. They have confiscated the unregistered diamonds."

"So what happens now?"

"You will accompany me to police headquarters and plead guilty to possession of the tickets."

"I'm allowed to have blank tickets."

"These appear to be from a stolen batch."

"So? That doesn't mean I stole them."

"I know, but dealing with our authorities becomes a matter of negotiation. Some charge had to be leveled. Stolen tickets or blood diamonds? I chose the lesser of two evils."

Vera Cruz harbored intense dislike for the Napoleonic pomposity of the tiny man, but couldn't help being impressed with his logic. "How astute of you. However, you do know I'm a pilot. Will there be a charge of some sort on a permanent record?"

"I believe the diamonds have taken care of that. But should you wish to revisit Italy, your entrance will be denied."

The captain smiled. He wasn't bothered about re-entering the country. He'd spent his life slipping through far more stringent immigration authorities than those in Italy.

CHAPTER THIRTY-TWO

When a persistent ringing woke Alex, she was in two minds whether to acknowledge it. It was probably her family who'd called every holiday since her husband died. They wanted to let her know she wasn't alone, which she was, make sure she was eating right, which she wasn't, and remind her not to work too hard, which was out of her control. They never seemed to give any thought to whether their enforced geniality and attempts at lifting her spirit made matters worse. In years past it had been easy to patiently explain she'd come to terms with the solitary personal life led by most airline people. An existence that those on a nine to five, Monday through Friday schedule, would never understand. But today Alex was in no mood, for this year she knew their concerns were founded in fact. With Vera Cruz God knows where, in who knows what condition, and Jake deliberately avoiding her, her life did feel hopelessly out of control. In fact, she felt a hundred times worse than any of her family could ever imagine, and there seemed no way to make things better.

The phone rang on, jarring her nerves like a toothache. Whoever was calling had no way of knowing she'd only slept four hours after the late arrival of an Air Malta flight the night before. So she waited for the answering machine to pick up. It did not. With the ringing in her head reverberating, Alex's resolve evaporated. She picked up the handset. "Hello."

"Hello yourself. Remember me?"

Of course she remembered him. Her body had craved him every waking second since he left her at the railway station. "My God, Tayo, I thought I'd never hear from you again. Are you okay? Why haven't you called? Where are you?" She hoped he was outside her door or at the airport as he'd so often been in the past.

"Whoa, hold on, let's do one thing at a time. Did you miss me?"

"You know I did. Where have you been, I'm crazy with worry imagining you're sick, or dead in a ditch."

"I'll tell you about that later. But first, I couldn't forget my favorite girl at Christmastime. I missed you and needed to hear your voice." Vera Cruz paused. "I also wanted to let you know I'm thinking about you, but probably won't see you until the New Year."

"Those bastards can't even give you a day off for Christmas?"

"This time it's not work. I'm in a bit of trouble, and if you can, I need your help."

"Of course I'll help, do I have to pick you up somewhere?"

"I'm in Rome."

"I'll fly over. We'll spend Christmas in one of The Palacio's giant beds."

"Tempting, but not possible. I got into a traffic accident and banged my head. It was nothing serious for me, but the other driver was hurt badly and it was my fault."

"I've seen Italians drive. They must have accidents all the time."

"I know, but listen, that isn't important. What is important is that when I got to the police station, they discovered my passport had expired. It's not simply a case of deporting me with a fine. Unless I get a new passport, I'm going to jail."

"My God, what can I do?"

"Get me a passport."

"How can I get you a passport? You need signatures, photos, proof of birth, all sorts of stuff."

"Don't worry, silly, I have a new passport. I left it in my other flight bag. But the idiots at crew reporting sent it God knows where, and only just found it in some backwater lost and found. It's now back at Heathrow waiting to be picked up."

"If it gets you home sooner I'll go get it. But how will I clear it through customs, I presume it's locked?"

"Crew control told me it's already been cleared. All you need do is take it home, break the locks, and send me the passport. Could you do that for me? I'd be so grateful."

"How grateful?"

"Get me back there and you'll find out."

"Umm. Sounds promising."

"One last thing, Alex. You need to talk to Ken in GAP's lost and found. He's been sorting out the mess and has the paperwork."

"Okay, Ken it is. Where do I send it?"

"Send what?"

"Wow, you did get a bang on the head—the passport."

"I'll call in a couple of days after I've arranged for one of the guys to carry it over."

"I'll bring it over."

"I've been in jail for six days, you're not seeing me like this."

"I didn't know you were so vain."

"There's a lot you don't know about me."

"Now there's an understatement."

"I know—I'm a rotten friend, but please, do it my way. I'll make it up to you. Now get off the phone. The sooner this gets done, the quicker I can be out of here."

Before Alex could say anything, a hollow click turned to static buzz. She spent several seconds clinging to the handset drawing solace from every microsecond of closeness their electronic reunion brought. She'd wanted to ask so much, but he'd sounded so desperate for help. She hadn't the heart to tackle him. No matter, there would be time enough for questions when she got him out of Rome. She replaced the handset. Christmas would no longer be as painful as she expected.

CHAPTER THIRTY-THREE

When Vera Cruz called his villa in Ericeira, Pete was waiting. "Hi, boss," he said. "What happened? I saw the cops offload you and the bag. And when I called PIA they said you'd been offloaded to take care of some family emergency. I knew that was crock, so where are you?"

"Still in Rome."

"You get arrested?"

"Sort of, some shit-head in Karachi tipped off the cops but the useless dagos here have no clue what's going on. Franco and his lawyer called in some favors but couldn't stop me getting busted for the tickets. I'm under house arrest at Franco's villa."

"So leave now, what are you waiting for?"

"Cops have everything I need to split. But like we planned, they can't pin anything on me. Hopefully I'll be out of here before they put two and two together."

"You want me to come over? You have a passport at Red's house and I could get lefty to rush through some ID."

"No, the sentencing hearing is on December twenty-third. It'll be over by the time you get organized."

"December twenty-third, that's cutting it fine. Will you go straight to the UK?"

"That would be my choice. But word is, immigration will kick me back to Karachi."

"Why Karachi?"

"Because like a dumb-ass, I traveled PIA, so I used my Pakistani passport. They say I'll get my cash back in Karachi, but I'm not holding my breath on that. In the meantime, I'm sitting here getting fat when I should be delivering that goddamn film."

"Is the bag clear?"

"It will be."

"So I'll meet you in Karachi?"

"Yeah. Franco started the ball rolling on my new identity, but you know what a crapshoot that place is. I'm not sure what more I'll need until I get there. I know one thing though—I'm not hanging around a day longer than necessary. That film has got to be delivered."

"I hear you. I'll hit the road today. You need anything from here?"

"No, but keep your eyes open. Somebody is getting uncomfortably close."

CHAPTER THIRTY-FOUR

Europa, like most airlines, asked for volunteers to work the holidays, and Alex selected the ten-to-six swing shifts on both Christmas Eve and Christmas Day. They were the same shifts as Ken in GAP's lost and found, and afforded her two opportunities to pick up Vera Cruz's bag.

Christmas Eve started bitterly cold, the sky dominated by huge sun-lit cumulonimbus clouds. Snow was not far off as Alex loaded a pile of family gifts into the car. She hoped the white stuff would hold off until after her shift and the drive to her parents for their traditional gift exchange.

*

As if the Gods were on Alex's side, all flights came and went on time. The shift flew by, and the Christmas spirit had magically transformed even the most staid of the airport's staff into happy purveyors of joviality. Now, at just after six, the airport was inundated with off-duty employees wandering from one festive gathering to another. Most extravagant was always the customs party, where liquor confiscated over the previous year was put to good use, and though she was stopped several times and invited to join the party, Alex had her evening planned. As soon as she had cleared Vera Cruz's bag, she was off to her parents. She made her way back to passenger handling to sign off.

It was six-fifteen when she pulled her timesheet, and in the place she usually logged her departure, someone had stuck a post-it. "Pigeonhole" was written on it. Intrigued, Alex signed out and hurried to her mail slot in the employee lounge. There, she found a small, brightly wrapped box, with a card reading, "from your Secret Santa." She knew nothing about a grab, so Alex decided not to open the gift immediately. It would probably reveal who sent it, and she hadn't the time to find them and say thank you. She dropped the box in her shoulder bag, and headed for the bus to terminal three.

*

The long haul terminal appeared deserted, and at GAP's lost and found, a clock wall hanging indicated "Ken will be back at six-fifteen." It was 6:35.

For a moment, it crossed Alex's mind to find the file in the computer and process the bag, however she knew such behavior outside one's own airline was totally unethical. But her day had gone so smoothly, it annoyed her that at the eleventh hour Ken had let her down. Chances were good he was partying somewhere not too far away, so she conspicuously paced, hoping he might be watching.

Ten minutes passed as Alex stood alone. She could hear throbbing party music in the distance and knew he might not return at all. She checked her watch again. Time was getting short. She'd promised to be at her mother's by seven-thirty, and being a stickler for punctuality, particularly for the family gift exchange, Alex reluctantly accepted she'd have to collect the bag another day.

Distracted by disappointment, and eager to be on her way, Alex turned quickly and collided with a baggage agent. His badge proclaimed him to be Ken.

She stepped aside to avoid further accident. "Jeez, man, where did you spring from?"

"Binnonabreak."

"I can see that. I'm Alex. I was told you have a flight bag belonging to Captain Vera Cruz."

"Thure do cathew," he slurred. "Wherzauthorization?"

"Authorization? He's my friend, why do I need authorization?"

"Woona want it to fall into the wrong handth."

"Excuse me?"

"You know—" He moved close and tapped the side of his nose.

"Good grief, check my ID. That's as good as it gets."

He teetered slightly as he looked at the ID attached to her pocket. "Alexth Mack, thoundth good, letth go."

"Are you still on duty?"

He gave her a lopsided grin, and opened the lock-up. "I'm entitled to a glath of thumthing . . . you do know ith Chrsthmas Eve?"

"Yes I do, now can we make this quick? I have an appointment."

"Betchya do. Piloth get all the good chikth."

Despite being imbued with alcohol, Ken efficiently adjusted the computer inventory, pulled the flight bag from lock-up, and handed Alex a wad of customs paperwork.

"You thure you wooden like a little drinkie?"

"Thank you, no." Alex threw the bag on a waiting cart, and trundled away from the tipsy agent.

When she arrived in customs' "something to declare," it too was deserted. However, she knew inspectors were in the office on the mezzanine floor above. She stood at the desk for several minutes before impatience overtook her, and she picked up the extension. Someone answered, and when his face popped into view at the window, she waved her paperwork.

"Need a bag cleared," she snapped into the phone.

"Late shift hasn't arrived, you'll have to wait."

"It's a crew bag. Can't you come down for five minutes?"

"No can do, I'm off duty."

Realizing she'd get further with honey than vinegar, her attitude softened. "Please, please, please, it's Christmas. Unless I get it cleared, I can't join the party."

"This party?"

"Maybe."

"I'll be right down."

When the mezzanine door opened flooding the area with music, the customs officer teetered down the stairs.

"Well, hello sweet-cakes," he said, smiling broadly. "What brings such a pretty lady to our neck of the woods?"

She pointed down. "Bag?" Her tone was tinged with sarcasm. "It would be nice if I could get it cleared this year."

He took Alex's paperwork. "Ooooh, in a hurry are we? I'd better get to it then." It took him a couple of attempts to sign on to his computer. Then he hastily looked at the bag's seal and checked its tag number against the bar code. "You know, the party could use a good-looking gal like you. Are you coming up for a drink?"

"I'm driving."

"Don't worry about that, most of the traffic cops are upstairs."

"Have somewhere else to go."

"You won't get a better mix, I'm telling you. We have some choice booze this year, champagne and everything. You look like a bubbly drinking sort of gal to me. Come on, one little drink. I gave you five minutes, return the favor."

"I thought clearing bags was your job."

"It's Christmas Eve, loosen up a bit."

"I think you're loose enough for the both of us. Could you please hurry, I'm supposed to be at my parents'."

"How sweet, Christmas with the folks. You're not married then?"

"That's none of your business. Can we get on with this?"

"My, my my, frosty. You definitely need warming up. Sure I can't persuade you to share one little champers for the road?"

"You're not the type I'd want to share anything with."

"Now that's just rude. For your information, missy, I was supposed to finish at six. I came down here as a favor, a Christmas

Eve favor, from me to you. You could've been waiting until my relief arrives, so you better be a bit nicer to me."

"Look, either clear the bag or send it back to lock-up. Or maybe I should call the watch commander?"

"Okay, okay, I get it, your loss."

*

The customs officer stamped her papers several times and handed them back. And as he watched her walk through the automatic doors, he fantasized about what a nice present she would've been under his Christmas tree. Then, intending to waste no more time getting back into the holiday spirit, he lobbed his paperwork into the "out" bin, ignored the flashing screen, and closed the file.

CHAPTER THIRTY-FIVE

As Alex approached Blake House, her parents' rambling Victorian lodge in the middle of town, it was resplendent with Disney-like Christmas lights. Even a mature conifer at the drive's entrance was ablaze, as each year her father found a reason to increase the illumination. She knew her mother begged him not to attempt to best the previous year's display, but he said people from miles around came to see his efforts, and carolers from the local church started their route at Blake with mince pies and a hot toddy, so it was expected.

Pulling into the drive, Alex sighed. She was a good deal more low-key in her approach to the Christmas festivities. Nevertheless, she knew the madness would soon sweep her up. It wasn't that she hated Christmas per se; it was simply that along with the jarring brilliance of the illuminations, which almost required eye protection to look upon, the annual gift exchange brought out the rambunctious worst in her brothers' busload of children. So she would do as she always did. Tamp down her inner Scrooge and bail at the first opportunity. It could be worse. She could be looking forward to another year alone. Instead, she had Vera Cruz's bag with the all-important passport, and the ghost of Christmas future promised good things.

Sitting quietly in her parents' drive, Alex breathed deeply and counted to ten. Then, fully composed and ready to face the inevitable outpouring of emotion from her parents, five brothers, their wives and twelve children, she gathered her first load of gifts.

*

As expected, the reunion proved to be a whirlwind of news and family information. But Alex's most awkward moments invariably occurred in the "fix up Alex" session which followed.

The badgering had started on the second Christmas after her husband's death, and always occurred in the same way. Gifts were separated into piles, ready for each to open on Christmas morning, the kids were put to bed, and the men retired to the billiard room. The ladies were then left to "chat," and one sister-in-law or the other always produced a list of ideal husband-candidates for Alex's consideration. They'd never accepted she had a singularly different way of living her life, and she constantly fought against fitting into a mold of their creation. She couldn't imagine what they'd make of the cavalier attitude of a man like Vera Cruz, so she was absolutely sharing no details about him. She simply accepted the names and phone numbers with as much grace as she could muster, and would later dispatch them to the trash.

By ten, eyelids drooping, and nerves on the wrong side of frazzled, Alex was ready to return to the peace and tranquility of her cottage. The family was used to her erratic schedule, and knowing she was working on Christmas Day, didn't try to delay her leaving. With crushing hugs, bags full of gifts, and food, she and her mother headed for the door.

As Alex pulled aside the heavy velvet curtain, additional insulation in the century old house, a chilling draft wafted their way. Then, as the front door swung open, the hallway flooded with a swirling icy blast and a wild flurry of snow. Having threatened all day, the heavy cotton ball flakes were now coming down at a good clip, promising Alex an arduous drive home. But home was where she intended to go. Pulling her collar about her ears, she kissed her mother, put her head down, and ventured to the car. However, within two steps of the porch, the brightness of the house's lights revealed the car had a flat tire.

*

Heavy drifting snow and lack of familiarity with her mother's vehicle made Alex's drive home a concentrated nightmare. She was exhausted as she activated her garage door and carefully steered her mother's larger sedan inside. And as she checked the trunk, which barely escaped being struck, she realized Vera Cruz's bag was still in her car. Alex cursed aloud. Having gone to so much trouble to pick up the bag it was now forty miles away. She'd intended to put his passport on the first available flight; now, until she got her car back, it was going nowhere.

Fighting tears, Alex carried her bags into the kitchen, unceremoniously dumped them on the counter, and called her mother.

Mrs. Blake told Alex the tire couldn't be fixed until after Christmas, and that one of her brothers would drop the car at the airport sometime during the evening of the twenty-seventh.

*

Alex's shift didn't start until noon on Christmas Day; nevertheless, she woke early. Taking coffee, two of her mother's brandy-laced mince pies, and her family's gifts, she settled into an armchair in front of a roaring fire.

As she opened each package, refolding and setting aside the gift-wrapping, it was clear they'd gone to a great deal of trouble selecting expensive practical gifts for the working woman. Just once it would have been nice to receive something totally useless. Something she could joke about for the next twenty years. Something she could put on the mantle and smile about every time it caught her eye. She set the gifts aside and worked on her second mince pie. Then she remembered her Secret Santa.

Inserting her feet in the cozy shearling slippers she'd just received, Alex shuffled to the hall, pulled the small, brightly wrapped package from her bag, and returned to the lounge. She finished her breakfast, then, in an attempt to guess what was inside, shook the package. There was no rattle, swoosh, or otherwise identifiable sound. She removed the outer paper revealing a small white cardboard box. She flipped the lid and found an oval object further wrapped in tissue paper. She smelled it—no detectable perfume. She shook it again, no sound. Her anxious fingers tore off the gauzy wrapping, which she never saved, and she was left with the swirling blizzard of a snow globe.

The smooth glass ovoid, sensually tactile and nestling perfectly in the indent of her cupped hand, had its face surrounded with crystals. And she noted the snowflakes weren't white, but a twinkling aurora borealis of color. Moreover, as the opalescent snow slowly settled, a tiny black vehicle emerged, on which half a dozen Keystone Cops were desperately clinging. It was totally useless, absolutely silly, and quite the most perfect gift she'd ever been given. It warmed her senses and tore at her heart, for she knew exactly who her Secret Santa was.

CHAPTER THIRTY-SIX

Everyone enjoyed working on Christmas Day. Loads were light, passengers came and went in good spirits, and the airline provided a lavish buffet on which the terminal's staff grazed throughout the day. The duty cops from Special Branch appeared in the early evening, and though hoping to patch up her misunderstanding with Jake, Alex was told he was working out of town. She decided to call him and thank him for the snow globe when she got home.

Alex was halfway home when heavy snow began to fall. But to her surprise, when she pulled onto Mulberry Lane, clearly defined tire tracks led toward her cottage. She beamed, imagining Vera Cruz had somehow made it back to England as a Christmas surprise. Her hopes were dashed as she rounded the corner to her garage and found no other car.

Taking a composing breath, Alex pulled cautiously into the garage. There, etched deep into the snow, on a path to and from the front door, were footprints. Intrigued, she bypassed the garage entrance to the house and made the snowy trek to the front door's vestibule. The auto light popped on, revealing a huge gift basket of very expensive toiletries.

With all concern for the cold gone, Alex stripped her hands of gloves and removed the basket's snow spattered envelope. It contained a gold embossed, deckle-edged card reading, "Thank you for getting my bag, see you soon." She was beside herself with joy, kissed the small white card, and wrestled the substantial basket into the kitchen.

The hypnotic blinking of her message machine punctuated the dark of the house. Without wasting time to turn on lights, Alex perched her gift on the counter and hit the play button.

Emotion overcame her upon hearing his voice. Leaning close to the machine, she closed her eyes and cherished the sound of every syllable.

"Hi you," Vera Cruz said. "Merry Christmas. I called to let you know I'm thinking of you, and hope you like the gift. I got word you picked up my bag. Thanks so much for that. And I have good news and bad. The good: forget about sending me the passport, the embassy came through. The bad: I have to make a detour to Karachi. I'll see you before the New Year though, I promise. Hold on to my bag until I get there."

Alex had never been so happy and sad all at once.

CHAPTER THIRTY-SEVEN

Along with every other airport department, Christmas traffic through customs had been light. Moreover, with Heathrow still in party mode, it was after eleven p.m. on the twenty-sixth before the late shift clerk got around to filing paperwork from the twenty-fourth and twenty-fifth. She understood why nobody had checked the bins as they went along, because there weren't many files. However, as she leafed through them, one record set off a mental alarm.

On the face, it appeared to be a regular misrouted crew bag, but when her anxiety wouldn't rest, she keyed the case number into her computer and reopened the file. She couldn't ignore the flashing. And the red tag assigned to this particular property had received no follow-up action.

As the clerk contemplated the potential for a serious breach of security, more than a little panic accompanied her tapping fingers. She double-checked the barcode—the alert had definitely not been acknowledged. Not wishing to make matters any worse, she brought the breach to the duty officer's attention. Within minutes, he'd informed the watch commander, and Officer Frank Paddock, a twenty-five year veteran of the customs service, received the type of midnight phone call no one in a security based position likes to receive.

*

"Officer Paddock, thank you for coming," said Jake.

"Did I have a choice?"

"No, but please sit. I'm Detective Inspector Fowler, Special Branch, this is Sergeant Tate."

"Special Branch? What's this all about?"

"We're here to get some information on a red flag bag you released at around six-thirty on Christmas Eve and didn't action. Do you know what a red flag means?"

Paddock shot Jake a what-sort-of-a-dumb-shit-do-you-think-I-am look. "What am I, a rookie, of course I know what a red flag means."

Jake held up a file. "Then why didn't you action this one on Christmas Eve?"

"Didn't realize I had one."

A highly suspect bag on the loose, and the lateness of the hour, did nothing to improve anyone's disposition. Tate stepped forward. "Didn't realize, or were too distracted?"

"What's that supposed to mean?"

"I know your shift and others were up on the mezzanine partying."

"What are you, some sort of spy? Everyone was partying. It's Christmas, there were no flights, ergo no passengers, so—"

"You had a drink or two?"

"Everyone had a drink or two. Oh, excuse me, except you."

"We get it," said Jake. "Just relax, Paddock. So did this bag accidentally slip by you, or did you ignore it for a reason?"

"For a reason? What are you getting at?"

"Nothing, yet. Think back, it's around six-thirty."

"Well, first, I'm not sure what bag you mean. How am I supposed to remember every bag I handle?"

"Ordinarily I'd have to agree with you. But this was Christmas Eve, and by your own admission the place was deserted. This was a pilot's flight bag, came out of lock-up, orange tag with the red."

"Oh shit." The look on Paddock's face said it all. "Yeah, I do remember it. I was supposed to be relieved at six, and at six, I poured myself a Scotch, a large one. Chugged it down pretty quick, after all, it was a party. Then I started on another, and one of the guys told me Rogers was going to be late. I figured that was no big deal, because the place was empty, with no incoming flight until nine-thirty. Then suddenly I see this passenger chick in 'something to declare' waving a fistful of docs at me. Nice looking, tall, dark hair, good legs."

Tate interjected. "Can we stick to the point? Did you see her on duty earlier in the day. Did you know her?"

"Don't think so. I'm normally in terminal one or I would've known who she was. I was helping out here. You know how it is at Christmas. Us old guys fill in so the guys with young kids can be home. I admit to having a couple of drinks, even asked her to join us upstairs. But when she got all huffy; I was more interested in getting back to the party. She was staff; I thought the bag was hers. It wasn't deliberate. I'm sorry. I wasn't paying attention and screwed up."

It was clear to Jake that despite his years on the job, the man before him had no concept of the importance of red flags. "You might think it was simply inattention, but your little screw up could prove disastrous."

"Disastrous? It was a crew bag. What the hell would a crew-member want to get by us, an extra pack of Marlborough?"

"You really have no idea what you—"

"Fowler!" interrupted Tate.

Jake softened. "Would you recognize her if I showed you a picture?"

"You bet, good-looking piece. Told you, I tried to get her to the party, but she was frosty, man. That's the kinda woman you want to—"

"All right, we get the picture." Jake motioned to Tate, who stepped out of the room, returned with the employee mug-shot book, and set it in front of the officer. "Go through this and identify who it was you dealt with."

Tate slowly turned the pages, until Paddock slapped down his hand. "Whoa, whoa, there, go back, again, one more. That's her, there she is."

Jake's heart was in his mouth. "Are you sure? Look again. No doubt in your mind, that's the girl?"

Paddock paused. "Yep, that's her, see those eyes, incredible blue, look like lenses, but I bet they—"

"Quiet," snapped Jake. "I'm finished with you for now. Report to the watch commander, I'm sure he has a few words for you."

Rising sheepishly, Paddock headed for the man who could really make his life a living hell.

As the door closed, Tate looked quizzically at her boss. "What's up? You look like you've seen a ghost."

Jake wished he had. It wouldn't be nearly so shocking as seeing his beloved Alex innocently staring from the page of plastic faces. It took a couple of minutes to shake off Jake, and return to Detective Inspector Fowler. "It's Alex Mack, Tate. I know her, and well, we are—"

"God, she's not a girlfriend, please don't tell me that."

"Not a girlfriend exactly. But someone very special who I respect. This is crazy; she wouldn't intentionally get involved in this business."

"Fowler, you know the score, you have to pass. You're too close. It'll go bad, it always does. You have to hand it over to someone else. You can't be impartial anymore, it's too difficu—"

"Don't lecture me on what I can and can't do. This is a misunderstanding. Whatever happened, there's a logical explanation, and when I talk to her, she'll tell me what it is."

"Okay, okay. Don't get all bent out of shape. You're the boss and we'll do it your way." Tate flipped the back of Alex's photo to reveal her address and other personal details. "Rose Cottage, Mulberry Lane, Weston-under-Wetherley. Whoa, that's way in the boonies. Do we go talk to her now?"

"No, it wouldn't serve any purpose. Supposedly Ms. Mack has

had the bag over twenty-four hours. It's either still with her, in which case we shouldn't tip our hand until the owner shows up. Or she's already passed it on, in which case she's our main lead, and we'll monitor her movements. Either way, I know she's not due back at work for a couple of days. Go home and get a couple of hours sleep, we'll go over later."

*

On a bright frosty morning, around nine-thirty, Jake and Tate pulled alongside the unmarked police car positioned at the end of Mulberry Lane. The officer in-situ told them he'd seen no movement since he arrived, and confirmed a twenty-four hour surveillance roster had been set up until further notice. Nodding approval, Jake and Tate continued to Alex's end of the lane, and stopped in front of a snow-blanketed cottage.

Constructed of old Cotswold stone, and backlit by the morning sun, the cottage glowed warm yellow against the bright blue sky. Surrounded by a low dry-stone wall, the property of over an acre was dotted with mounds of pristine white, under which shrubs were lying dormant. Standing sentinel on either side of the front door, shiny green rhododendrons, leaves curled tight against the cold, waited for Mother Nature's orders. It looked like a *Currier and Ives* watercolor and Jake raised an eyebrow. Despite his long friendship with Alex, he'd never been to the cottage, and could only imagine how much more beautiful the garden must be ablaze with spring and summer colors.

"Wow, this is some spread," said Tate, as they walked to the gate. "Rich kid, I guess?"

"No," said Jake. "Nothing like that."

"What then?"

"The cottage belonged to her husband's family. It became hers after he died."

"Right, you know that because she's a friend of yours."

"Don't go there, Tate."

"Just saying. So, apart from her being an eligible young widow, what else do you know?"

He gave her "the look." "My research indicated she has an extensive investment portfolio, a healthy bank account, and an excellent salary from her job with Europa."

"So why would she be involved in this crap? She certainly doesn't need the money."

"My point exactly."

"And you didn't share this with me last night because?"

"Because I didn't know. Until I did the search, I had no idea just how wealthy she was. We're friends, and friends don't ask those questions. Now look at me. Some friend. I've invaded her space on a financial as well as personal level."

"If she's a real friend, you'll explain the situation and she'll see the logic."

"Oh yeah, and how will that go? Hi, Alex, this is my partner, sergeant super-spy-at-the-airport Tate. We know you cleared a bag of contraband through customs to give to your boyfriend who's a world-class cheat, liar, and felon. And, keeping it real, if you're in it just to get laid, there are plenty of non-losers in the ocean. 'Cause we know you're not involved in this smuggling business for the money—you have a boat load. And, oh yeah, by the way, I came by all this information totally by accident. So can we still be friends because I'm a cop just doing my job."

Tate winced. "Holy mother. Take it away boss, I'm right behind you."

Jake's heart and head were in turmoil. It had been months since their initial misunderstanding about the captain in the coffee shop. That had been forgiven. Then at Java Julia's, upon hearing Alex had special feelings for Vera Cruz, he'd retreated before saying anything hurtful. Since then they'd spoken, and he'd tried to warn her about the pilot, but clearly he hadn't gotten through to her. Now, though his investigations during his time in Europe allowed him to address the captain's bona fides with more authority, his official appearance at her house would confirm his invasive delving into the most private aspects of her life. It might be essential to his investigation, but he knew it would drive an immovable wedge of mistrust between them.

As he wrestled with the dictates of his heart, and the cold, hard, facts in his head, Jake realized Alex's involvement in anything illegal disturbed him on two distinctly different levels. On one hand, his heart knew her history had given her enormous inner strength, and on some level that personality trait might lead her to crave the excitement a man like Vera Cruz could provide. On the other, his head told him she was a wealthy young woman with no motive for doing any of the things of which she was suspected. She was, however, ripe to be hoodwinked by a man like Vera Cruz, who'd made his fortune playing off the emotional needs of lonely women.

A nod to Tate indicated Jake was ready to confront his friend. Cautiously approaching the front door, for he didn't entirely know how she would react to his arriving unannounced, he rang the bell.

A smiling, bathrobe-clad Alex, looking as serene as he'd ever seen her, opened the door. "Hello, Jake, are you and your friend lost?"

"No, Alex, we, that is Sergeant Tate and I, have some questions we'd like to ask you." Jake motioned to Tate, who already had her ID out.

"This looks official, you better come in."

*

Tate chose to remain standing, while Jake sat on one of the sofas opposite Alex. "We're here to ask you questions about a bag you cleared through customs. It came from lock-up, and was released to you in error."

"A bag? You're Special Branch, what possible interest could you have in a bag?"

Tate piped in. "That's none of your concern right now."

Alex scowled. "Well, that put me in my place. What's this all about, Jake?"

Jake glared in Tate's direction and took a softer tone. "The bag, a pilot's flight bag, was given to you in error. We need to get it back, and we need to know who you're giving it to."

Because she knew him so well, Alex heard something odd in Jake's tone. "Umm, sounds to me like there's something more in what you're saying."

"It's a simple question, Alex."

Duplicity from so close a friend annoyed her, and she was immediately on the defensive. "It belongs to a friend, Jake. Remember? Those people you cherish, and trust, and do nice things for. What's this really about?"

Jake blushed. "Just a routine inquiry on a bag we think holds contraband."

"I have no idea what 'routine inquiry' means, but the bag was handed to me from lock-up with a customs clearance tag, meaning it had been searched. I carried it through 'something to declare' like I'm supposed to, where the officer could have gone through it again, but did not. Now you're telling me it may hold contraband, which clearly customs didn't find when they searched it in the lock-up. So now I ask myself, what it is you're not telling me?"

Jake looked at Tate.

"Your silence confirms there is something more to your inquiry. Do either of you want coffee? I just made some."

They declined.

"Well, I need a caffeine fix, so talk among yourselves 'til I get back."

Alex detected Jake's presence behind her and spun around. "What the hell's going on? You couldn't ask me about this at work? Why did you have to bring one of your police—persons—to my home? This isn't right, Jake. I thought we were friends and the first time you visit me here, it's as an enemy."

"Enemy? Is that what you think?"

"Yes, that's what I think. Why else would you bring her?"

"Her? What's she got to do with anything? You're reading all sorts of things into this."

"I'm reading what I see and feel into this. Why would a man I know and trust, who I've shared the deepest secrets of my life with, feel it necessary to bring along a female police officer? Do you intend to have her strip and cavity search me? My God, you only had to ask—I would've let you do that . . . for fun!"

"Alex, please, there's no need to be sarcastic."

"Oh, I think there is. I thought our friendship was special, important even. Then for no reason you leave me stranded in a coffee shop, where *you* invited me. You won't return my calls, and when you finally do honor me, I get a snotty lecture about someone I'm dating. Then there's that cryptic message about not calling unless it's life or death. You relegated me about as low as I can go, Jake. *You* relegated *me*. Then I get the snow globe, and I think we're back to where we were. The next thing I know, you're invading my home with Miss Robocop out there, acting all ID card flashing, business official, accusing me of God knows what."

"Sweetie." Jake leaned in close and whispered. "We seem to have had a series of huge misunderstandings, which can't be resolved now. Tate is just one of my team. We're not here to do anything intense. We're just asking questions. I'm sorry if you feel I have in some way betrayed you, but—"

She pushed him away. "Betrayed me? I feel like you've kicked me in the teeth. You know me. My God, I've bared my soul to you. How could you accuse me of trying to smuggle anything important enough to involve Special Branch? I know what your department does, Jake, remember? I also work at the airport."

"Then you know it's not about smuggling. I don't give a damn if your friend didn't pay duty on some expensive trinket he's carrying. This bag belongs to someone who is part of a chain of—" Jake suddenly cut off. "I'm sorry, I can't tell you any more right now."

"Well, Mr. So-Called Friend, if you can't tell me what you mean, I won't tell you anything, either." Alex picked up her coffee and returned to the sitting room.

Tate was walking around the room assessing her possessions. "Nice stuff," she said when she spotted Alex.

"Nice, and for the most part very expensive—you break it, you bought it."

Tate ignored the edge and continued to mooch. She stopped at a snow globe, set in a prominent place on the mantelpiece. She shook it, covering the tiny policemen with multi-colored snowflakes. "Hey, boss, don't you have one exactly like this on your desk?"

Before Jake could answer, Alex walked over and snatched back her globe. "You're mistaken, Sergeant. This is one of a kind, there will never be another like it. It came with special feelings from a very dear friend who disappeared one afternoon. I'm not sure I'll ever see him again."

*

As Tate continued roaming, Jake realized he'd made a huge mistake in not handing over this part of his investigation to someone else. Nevertheless, now that he'd started and was about as low as he could be in Alex's estimation, he saw no reason to bail. "Alex, I'm sorry, but now my inquiry is official. I need that bag; please bring it to me."

She sipped from her cup without a glance in his direction. "Don't have it."

Tate stopped her property review, came alongside Alex, and hovered menacingly over her chair. "Where is it?"

"My friend has it."

"Do you mind if I look around?" said Tate.

"Look around? I think you've done quite a lot of that already. Go right ahead, I have nothing to hide." With Tate in another room, Alex turned on Jake. "Now she's gone, are you going to tell me exactly what you're looking for and who this bag is supposed to belong to?"

"I think the bag belongs to a rogue pilot called Vera Cruz." Jake took a deep breath. "His sideline to flying is smuggling things— money, precious gems, drugs . . . whatever someone will pay him to carry." He paused to let the information sink in. "I believe this bag holds something special."

Alex's face gave nothing away. "What do you mean 'special'?"

"Don't know for sure. I need to check the bag and talk to this Vera Cruz character."

"You make him sound like a monster."

"Maybe he is."

"He is nothing of the sort. Besides, I thought pilots were under constant scrutiny. Their airline, airport security, customs, the FAA, for God's sake. How could any of them get away with something like that?"

Jake had seen this contrary streak in Alex from time to time, and knew his inquiries would get no further. "Determined criminals can get around anything and anybody."

"You mean me."

"I didn't say that."

"You don't need to. Remember, I know you—or at least I thought I did."

Exasperated, Jake ran a hand through his hair. "Well, this is just going from bad to worse. I think we better leave, and give you some time to think about what I said. If you want to talk to me, day or night, you know where to find me."

"Be still my heart, I have an open invitation to talk to you."

"Really not fond of the sarcasm, Alex. Tate, let's go, you're not going to find anything."

*

As they climbed into the car, Tate put a hand on Jake's arm. "I know she's your friend and all, but she's holding back."

"Yeah, and I think you're right."

"Hallelujah, for once I'm right. Right about what?"

"Being too close. I've never seen her like that before. She hated me, and God knows if I'd have left you two alone, she'd have taken a carving knife to you."

"So what do we conclude from that?"

"Not only is she holding something back, I think she and Vera Cruz are seriously romantically involved. Though from his reputation, romance isn't exactly the right word."

"Well, that's gotta be tough for you."

"You think?"

"So bail."

"I can't now, especially when my gut is telling me she's lying. To me . . . who she's always been . . . damn, it doesn't matter now. She's stashed his bag somewhere. Contact France, Italy, Portugal, anywhere you can think of, and get updated mug shots of all four of our named pilots. Also, put out Alex's picture as a potential accomplice."

"Anything else?"

"Yeah," Jake said. "I need a drink. Where's the nearest pub?"

"It's not opening time yet. This is really getting to you, isn't it?"

"So, what are you saying, I told you so?"

"Would it help?"

"No."

"Then I'll shut up and do my job," Tate said.

"Thanks."

"For what?"

"Not busting my balls."

"Oh, that's gonna come. You hardly know me yet."

Jake smiled as he started the car. "You know, Tate, whatever Alex has done with that bag, I don't think we'll see it until Vera Cruz shows up. However, I do know that until I said something, she had no idea what her captain has been up to when he's not flying."

"Agreed. She doesn't seem the type to get deliberately involved in anything shady. She's way too . . . what's the word . . . virtuous."

CHAPTER THIRTY-EIGHT

When Vera Cruz arrived in Karachi, the microfilm delivery deadline loomed dangerously close. Nevertheless, his time at the airport deportation center was minimal. Greased palms ensured his immediate release, and he received a lecture on expected behavior, and an envelope from Franco. It contained ten thousand dollars, and a note.

It is clear, my dear Tayo, that it would not be in our family's best interests to encourage your return to Italy. Cousin Edmondo used the diamonds and cash to pay fines and legal costs, but understand: had you not had a major family responsibility outstanding, I would have left you high and dry. Use the money wisely; there will be no more. Rest assured that with or without your assistance, the family will go on, so to prevent us contacting you again, do what is expected. I trust you take my meaning.

Vera Cruz tore the note into tiny pieces. Whatever mayhem occurred, Franco always emerged smelling like a rose. And while it used to bother him that the pompous bloodsucker simply reaped the benefit others risked their lives for, today he was indifferent. The film was his last delivery, and once he got to the UK and collected the agreed upon million dollars, he was retiring to Ericeira.

The prospect of that much money was a heady aphrodisiac, and as the captain hailed one of the cabs circulating the police station, he was in two minds whether to detour to his stewardess friend's apartment. Then he recalled she hadn't shown during his last visit. It was of no importance. For a man like him, there were plenty more willing bodies. Dropping the confetti of Franco's letter beneath the broom of a gutter sweeper, Vera Cruz climbed into a cab and told the driver to take him to the Intercontinental Hotel.

*

By the time Pete arrived on December twenty-seventh, his and Vera Cruz's passports, IDs, and business documents had been delivered. And, as dawn broke on December twenty-eighth, the captain and his associate made their way to the airport.

CHAPTER THIRTY-NINE

Unusually heavy snow was taking its toll on England's drivers. It hadn't warmed during the day, and though the fog was long gone, black ice lay in treacherous patches on the roadway. Alex drove home slowly, her foot hovering over the accelerator. This was one time she wished she had her mother's heavier sedan instead of her small sports car.

As she left the highway and hit deep country, hoar-frosted wires and petrified tree branches hung dangerously brittle in the moonlight and the occasional bomb of crusted ice exploded onto the road as the wind blew through. At any other time, crystallized water skimming atop jet-like tarmac might have been beautiful. But tonight Alex saw it as an accident waiting to happen. She drove on, summoning mind-numbing focus to avoid spinning on the slick surface. But within half a mile of home, even her extreme caution couldn't prevent the car from fishtailing at the approach to each intersection.

Setting her wipers to fast, Alex cursed. She'd prayed the snow hold off during her shift, to avoid dealing with delayed flights, but now it was coming down so thick and fast she wished she'd stayed at the airport for the night. With barely ten feet of visibility, she needed her last ounce of concentration to negotiate a snow-packed Mulberry Lane. She was so engrossed that she didn't think much of the vehicle parked off to the side of the road.

*

Thankful to be in the confines of her garage, Alex just sat in her car. She couldn't remember being so mentally drained, and knew it wasn't simply the harrowing drive home. Her life was spiraling out of control and there didn't seem to be a thing she could do about it. She took a deep breath, knowing a glass of wine would calm her, and opened the door. However, in her haste to be free of the car, she hadn't counted on stiffened arms and legs from the tension of the drive. Catching her foot on the clutch, she plunged headlong to the concrete. Her gloved hands took the brunt of her body's skid forward, but as she pulled herself upright, a large tear was evident around the zipper of her boot. Ordinarily, she'd have laughed at such clumsiness, but with her emotions in crisis and her nerves raw, tears welled. Cursing all men for being trouble-making bastards, Alex left Vera Cruz's bag in the trunk and limped into the kitchen.

The message machine was flashing and, lurching forward, she smacked the play button.

"Alex, it's Jake. I'm truly sorry. My God, it's all I seem to be saying to you lately. You have to believe me when I say I was simply doing what's right. Maybe it shouldn't have been me that intruded into your space, but as your friend, I was trying to do what is best for you. I was told remaining impartial was impossible, and I'm beginning to understand why. Can you forgive me? Is there something I can do, anything I can say to make things right with us? I miss our time together, I miss you, and I really need to see you. Can you call me now, no matter what time it is? I really need you to—"

Alex thumped the machine, cutting off Jake's message. "You don't need me for anything!" she yelled. "You're a sanctimonious bastard, and I hate you." She didn't even care about the pain in Jake's words because she was disappointed he wasn't Vera Cruz. As she stripped off her boots and flung them in a corner, she sank deeper into the dark place she had lately fallen.

After pouring a glass of wine, Alex put a match to the fire and settled on the sofa. It didn't matter that she was still in uniform and up impossibly late. Her emotions were in such a mess, she'd never sleep. And as she sipped the wine, letting the alcohol relax her, Alex realized that even after her husband died, she hadn't been reduced to such a crippling state of negativity. She was clearly addicted to the intense emotions Vera Cruz drew out of her, and the thought she might lose him brought her abject and profound misery. But why was she putting herself through this? It wasn't that the still small voice of reason hadn't repeatedly told her that an intelligent, worldly woman shouldn't be reduced to a sniveling wreck because her man wasn't around. So why didn't she simply let him go? Because even that voice's power couldn't negate whatever spell he'd cast over her. As deeply as his cavalier attitude hurt her, she was desperate to have him inside her.

As the fire and alcohol warmed her, Alex mellowed. And suddenly, it all became clear. She might be annoyed at Vera Cruz, but she was truly disappointed in herself. Disappointed she'd let any man manipulate her for even a short time. And she was angry about Jake's insinuations, but furious with herself. Furious that his suspicions might be right, and she'd been played for a fool.

Alex poured another glass of wine, and sitting at the kitchen table with her mind on idle, she stared blankly at the window made ebony by the winter's night.

The ringing phone shook her back to the present. She let it ring. Was it Jake with more placating protestations? She didn't want to deal with that right now. Or might it be Vera Cruz, telling her he was on his way? Well, screw him too. She was sick of being his bed warmer, sick of his power and his sexuality, sick of his self-absorbed world.

The jarring tone continued for so long Alex finally realized her careless swipe at the machine must have disengaged the message mode. She could simply wait for it to stop, but both the men in her life would keep trying until something or somebody answered.

She finger-tipped the handset, ready to facilitate its swift return to the cradle, should whomever it was say anything she didn't want to hear.

A worried voice drifted down the line. "Alex, it's Hugh." It was her neighbor at the farm next door. "Thank goodness you're there. Sorry to call so late, but I saw your lights go by, then when your answering machine didn't pick up you had me worried. Is everything okay over there?"

"Hugh, hi, yeah, everything's fine, sorry, I was distracted, what's up?"

"Call me paranoid, and you know I can be a bit out there, but do you have some crazy stalker boyfriend? 'Cause there's been a guy parked by the stile for a couple of days."

"You're kidding. I've no idea who it might be—have you spoken to him?"

"Yeah, went out this morning, had to, he could be a pervo, and I have Mattie and Jillie to consider. Anyway, he said he was doing a government survey. Right, like he would be down our lane in the middle of winter. He did look official though, was scribbling stuff on a clipboard, even had one of those fancy police radios on his dash."

"What the hell? Oh, hang on, was he a customs guy?"

"Don't know, can they do stuff away from the airport?"

"Sure." She knew exactly what was going on. "They can act just like the police, especially with airline staff. We're subject to spot checks, and there's a big flap on right now with so many people trying to slide by extra booze for the New Year."

"Oh right." He laughed. "I would never have thought of that."

"You know how airline people love to party."

"Well, he's barking up the wrong tree with you—you don't even drink, do you?"

"Special occasions, births, weddings, stuff like that."

"I bet that's who he is then."

"Don't worry, Hugh, I'll find out, and get back to you. Thanks for watching my back. Give Karen and the kids a kiss from me."

"What about me?"

"You just get a hug. Take care."

As she calmly replaced the handset, Alex was fighting mad. While Hugh might have bought the story about a customs spot check, she knew Jake had something to do with the man at the end of the lane. She could hardly believe he left a bogus apology message, knowing he had someone spying on her. He clearly had no intention of letting her live her life.

*

It was well past midnight when Jake's home phone rang.

"Hi, Alex," he said, wide-awake and not surprised to hear from her. "How are you?"

"Get that bloody snoop away from my house."

"Well, I'm glad you're all right too."

"Cut the crap, Jake! I'm as mad as I can possibly be, and about now you're the last person I give a damn about."

"Alex, what's happening? I've never known you so bent out of shape and angry about anything. What is this guy doing to you?"

"Leave him out of this. Just get your goon away from my house."

Vehemence wasn't what he expected, and her anger left him no alternative. "Tell me where your pet captain's bag is, and I'll help you out of this mess."

"Since when am I answerable to you for the company I keep? And what makes you think I'm in any sort of mess?"

"Look—"

"I don't have to look at anything. I don't even have to listen to what you have to say. Who the hell do you think you are?"

"Calm down, I'm just trying to protect—"

"Protect? Protect me from what? You're the only person I see pushing his nose where it's not wanted. Why would you think I need your bloody protection? Now before I say something we'll both regret, get your creep away from my house."

"Can't do that."

"Can't or won't? What is this, some B-grade movie where you follow me around, I wake up one morning and realize how much you love me, then fall simpering into your arms, begging your forgiveness? Well don't hold your breath, Mr. Policeman. You and the bozo at the end of the lane can go to hell."

"No one is going anywhere. I'm here and he's there for your protection."

"Aghh, are you not listening to me? I don't need protection. I don't need anything from you."

"But I need some things from you. Tell me where to find Vera Cruz, and give me his bag."

"I told you. I—DO NOT—HAVE IT! Are you so thick you're not hearing, or do you and your cronies get special training in intimidating innocent women?"

"That's enough, Alex. You don't know what you're saying. The surveillance stays until I get Vera Cruz and the bag."

"You . . . you . . . fucking creep. After all the time we've spent together, I don't believe you're doing this. Are you mad because he got to me before you did? Is that it, Jake? If you can't have me, nobody can?"

"I'm not the issue here. I want you to be happy, but not under these circumstances."

"There are no circumstances. You and your police donkeys are being bullies because the badge says you can."

"That's the stupidest thing you've ever said. I don't know what's happened to you, but this guy is not good for you. He's turned you into a—"

"Into a what, Jake? Tell me, give me a chance to respond."

"Quit the histrionics, you're being stupid and irrational."

"Typical cop. Because you don't like somebody's friends, you turn the country into a police state. Well I'm not going to sit quietly by and allow you and the other fascist pigs to lurk outside my house and spy on what I'm doing."

"You know, Alex, I've heard that kind of idiotic rhetoric many times before, but never from someone whose opinion I actually respect. I might not have said all the things I should before this particular shit hit the fan. But I think I've shared enough of myself that you know the very notion of that intractable dogma is abhorrent to me. You also know in your heart we're in the same place. I've been lonely, I can feel your pain, because I have it too, but you're fast approaching a place where I can't help you."

"I don't know how much plainer I can be. Screw the bag, and screw all you jack-boot wearing Nazis."

There were several seconds of ominous silence before Jake replied, "I didn't ever think I'd say this, but I don't know you anymore. And what's most disturbing about your sentiment is that such drivel invariably comes from someone who isn't sure they are a hundred percent right." There was no hiding the iciness in his tone. "You know me, you know where I'm coming from, and I thought we understood each other. God knows, by now you must know how much I love you, but this is too much. A long time ago, you told me you never lie, and if I didn't want an honest answer, don't ask the question. As it stands tonight, I believe this bag, and its owner, have made a liar out of you. I've tried to tell you in the gentlest way I can—Vera Cruz is dangerous, and what's in his bag could get you hurt, even killed. I put the officer outside the house for your protection, and while you might be floating on some sort of misconceived romanticized cloud about this pilot, at some point in the not-too-distant future, he will turn on you and you will need my help."

"I will nev—"

"Shut up and listen. I'm getting more information about Vera Cruz every day, and it's not good. You're a grown woman and you can do what you like, go where you like, be with whomever you like. But if you break the law, I'm going to step in. And I will arrest you. Surveillance is not something I take lightly, but if I put an officer outside your house, it means the information I've received is true, and you are in danger. If you don't believe what I'm saying, look in the bag." He paused to give her time to reply; she did not. "You must know he's using you for something. Ask yourself, where did he come from? Where does he go? Do I really know who he is?"

Expecting her to say something, he only heard a catch in her throat. He knew she was crying, but he couldn't stop now. "What do you and he have in common? What do you talk about? What future do you see with him? Alex, I know you think he cares for you, but I have evidence that you're not the only woman he's seeing."

"I know he sees other women." She sniffed back tears. "We talked about that, but not in England, we have an understanding, he—"

"He's lying to you. I have evidence he's drawing you inch-by-inch into something from which you will not escape. We have systems and people watchers at the airport; my God, you know that. But you were so taken in by this creep you ignored them. I was in Europe, I told you. The authorities there have pictures of you and Vera Cruz together in a car in Calais and Folkestone. We still have eyes on the car and its cargo. How much more I get to know is up to you."

"If you knew we were doing something wrong, why didn't you arrest us?"

"It's a trail, Alex; we gather information until we build a case. We watch the little guys who lead us to the paymasters. I had no idea how much you were involved until the customs officer identified you as the clearer of Vera Cruz's bag. We back-tracked from there. I couldn't then, and can't now, believe you know what is truly going on."

When Alex said nothing and shallow breathing echoed down the line, Jake knew she was more upset than he'd intended.

"Sweetie, please listen to me, I'm not here to upset you."

"Then why are you doing it?"

"Look, I shouldn't tell you what I'm about to, but I'm prepared to do anything to make you see what you've fallen into." He carefully weighed his words. "For some time police authorities all over Europe have been tracking the movements of a group of rogue pilots. Recently we discovered the group was the same person, the man you know as Tayo Vera Cruz. Now, simply by association, you are a part of some very dangerous activities. You don't have to be afraid to tell me what you've done, because I know in my heart you were doing things out of misplaced affection. But think about it calmly for just a minute. You know what we do at Special Branch, and this Vera Cruz business is a really big deal. I need to take a closer look at that bag, and I need you to help me find Vera Cruz. Believe me, I wouldn't put you in a danger if I couldn't protect you. And I've avoided telling you exactly what I suspect, because once you know, if you withhold information, you'll be in such serious trouble even I can't help you."

"I don't need—"

"Okay, you give me no choice. We at Special Branch and the authorities of Europe strongly suspect that somewhere in Vera Cruz's flight bag, hidden from a routine search, is a quantity of microfilm—"

"Oh please—microfilm—what are we, in some sixties James Bond movie? Criminals don't use microfilm these days, it's all digital downloads, coded memory sticks and encrypted whatever on the web."

"That's the beauty of these guys, they're going back to basics.

They know the authorities expect the other mediums. My God, we have whole departments of geeks whose only purpose is rooting out the technical stuff. We don't expect this."

"How convenient, Jake, you have an answer for everything."

"It's very important you believe me. This film not only contains the names of deeply embedded terrorist operatives, but also lays out deployment instructions that will help those individuals bomb dams and bridges in the United States. Do I need to say more? You know as well as I do, if that film gets into the wrong hands, thousands of innocent men, women ,and children will die."

He could hear her breathing more rapidly, and raised his voice. "Alex, I need you to understand the ramifications of what I'm telling you. You can't ignore what I've told you. I know you care. You have history, which makes you care. You need to help me with this. You need to tell me where the bag is, and you must tell me when and where you are next meeting Vera Cruz. Alex, are you listening to me?"

She said nothing.

"My God, woman, what is wrong with you? He doesn't love you. He's using you, why can't you see that? Alex, answer me, damn it. What is your obsession with this womanizing con man? You can't be that desperate."

As soon as he uttered the words, Jake knew he'd gone too far. With the finality of a prayer's amen, an empty black hole of static followed the severed connection. And with a roar of frustration and regret, he hurled his phone across the room.

*

Alex stared at the phone for some seconds, trying to absorb what Jake had said. With her mind a cloud of contradictions in a fog of disbelief, she fought for independence and concluded that what he'd said was a blatant act of spite from a jealous and bitter man.

199

Then in a microsecond of recall, she saw the honesty in his face, felt his gentle protective embrace, and remembered how they'd met. On that first day, at the grief center, when his unconditional understanding had bonded them in a way she couldn't begin to describe. She instinctively knew they'd be friends forever, and now she'd lost him. Paralyzed with confusion and regret, Alex sat and sobbed like a baby.

CHAPTER FORTY

No matter what time of year, Karachi is the pungent sweating armpit of the world, and Vera Cruz couldn't get out soon enough. He and Pete took separate cars to the airport—walking the last hundred yards, as an accident caused unexpected entertainment for the on-looking whirlpool of humanity. And now inside the terminal, there seemed to be twenty family members and friends attending to every person traveling. Everywhere rag-tag piles of baggage waited for check-in or were being repacked by those carrying overweight pieces. The only open space was in front of the first-class check-in desk.

Pete arrived first, disappeared into the sea of people, and took up his position in the KLM departure area. Vera Cruz won a hard fought battle through the milling crowds, half of whom appeared not to know why they were there or where they were going, and with only minutes to spare presented his first-class ticket at the PIA check-in desk. He had no worries that a recently deported individual such as he would bring attention to himself by traveling first class, because appropriate officials were paid handsomely to allow him to leave Pakistan. In spite of that, he knew that without a second thought, those very people would alert Heathrow's authorities that he was on the flight as soon as it was airborne.

Carrying only hand baggage and enough secondary documentation to convince a grand jury he was Mahatma Gandhi, Vera Cruz checked in as Mario Bonetti, a dealer in spices and exotic wood. The desk agent was, as always, extremely respectful to her first-class passenger, but Vera Cruz couldn't fail to notice her vaguely horrified expression as she recognized him from a picture he knew was in the desk's watch log. Not wishing to make her feel any more uncomfortable, he smiled warmly, knowing protocol dictated her next move.

Smiling sweetly, the clerk picked up the phone. "I apologize for the delay, Mr. Bonetti, but I believe my supervisor is holding a message for you."

Vera Cruz knew "holding a message" was a euphemism for "undesirable attempting to leave the country," and ordinarily security would now prevent his boarding. He smiled. "As long as they hold the flight."

"I don't know about that but . . . excuse me one minute." She spoke to her supervisor, then re-addressed Vera Cruz. "My mistake, sir, no message after all." She handed over the boarding pass. "Enjoy the flight, Mr. Bonetti."

Walking briskly through the VIP security and departure control, Vera Cruz arrived at the Heathrow gate area as they made the final boarding call. Next door, he saw passengers assembled for KLM's departure to Amsterdam thirty minutes later, and catching Pete's eye he nodded. Both men headed to the men's restroom and collided, resulting in both sets of boarding cards falling to the floor. With customary apologies, each picked up the other's boarding pass and moved on.

*

When a call rang out for "one remaining passenger on PK 286 to London's Heathrow Airport," Pete pulled out appropriate identification and hustled to the gate. He handed the passenger agent his documents, and disappeared down the gangway.

*

After swapping his ticket with Pete, Vera Cruz had proceeded to KLM's first-class lounge. There, he quietly sipped champagne until the attendant advised him of the last call for the flight to Amsterdam. Setting down his glass, he took out his alternative identification, walked directly to the gate, and boarded the flight.

CHAPTER FORTY-ONE

Jake was four-letter word spitting annoyed. With one phone call, which he'd anticipated would be a reconciliation, he'd lost his professional cool and managed to alienate Alex so entirely, there was little chance she'd ever talk to him again. He had arrogantly thought their history together and his honest plea for her to come to her senses would give her the confidence to lure Vera Cruz into a trap. However, he'd grossly underestimated her feelings for the pilot. And while his mind was absolutely clear what was needed to proceed with his investigation, it would take something he wasn't sure he possessed to re-establish his relationship with the woman he loved.

*

It was 7:30 a.m. when Jake arrived at his office. Eddie Barstow was already there.

"Whoa, mama," he said. "You look like you had an eventful night."

"I wish," said Jake, pouring coffee. "A crazy woman with skills might be worth how lousy I feel. Instead, it's this Vera Cruz shit keeping me awake. I got a message . . . they had him in Rome for a week! It seems they didn't give a shit about the warrant, just deported him back to Karachi with a slap on the wrist."

"It's not all bad. In fact, I was just about to call you and tell you."

"Tell me what?"

"On your desk, message from Karachi."

Jake found the note on his computer. "Well, I'll be. So that frigging bag is still here. He's coming to get it."

"And your girlfriend probably has it."

"Alex is not my girlfriend."

"Jake—it's me you're talking to. You want me back at her house with a crew?"

"Nah, it can wait, she's not going anywhere. Besides, after our screaming match last night she'll probably lodge a complaint with internal affairs, and I'll be back on the beat by noon."

"Now that's why you look like death warmed over."

"Yeah, like you're George Clooney."

Eddie laughed.

"Well there's no mistaking, this dude has balls," said Jake.

"Best place to hide is usually in plain sight."

"You think he's on to us?"

"My vote is yes."

"So he won't be using any of the names we know. We'll have to stake out the airport and pull in anyone who resembles our photos."

Eddie whistled. "Heathrow's a huge chunk of real estate."

"We'll narrow it down to flights leaving Karachi around the same time as the PIA."

"Sounds like a plan, I'll get a list together."

"You know what really bugs me, Ed?"

"Apart from tapioca, poodles, and disco?"

"I'm serious."

"You usually are."

Jake angrily flicked the note. "Countries that harbor men like Vera Cruz. I mean, these people wreak terror around the world, and are allowed to come and go relatively freely because some government official is paid off. And then, after the shit hits the fan, and because the world is watching, they get all righteous and spring into action."

"It's always been that way."

"Doesn't make it right."

"Never does, but we work around it. I'll get that list and meet you at PIA."

*

Armed with pictures and a description of their man, Heathrow's Special Branch and the local constabulary were out in considerable numbers. With instructions to ignore passport and ID names, their mandate was to detain anyone who remotely fit Vera Cruz's description.

So, as the PIA flight from Karachi landed and its passengers disembarked, officers positioned themselves at several points along the route to immigration. PIA's liaison officer, Jake, and Eddie Barstow—the only local agent to have seen Vera Cruz face-to-face—remained in the gate lounge. However, by the time passenger handling advised them all passengers were clear of the aircraft, Barstow has seen no one he felt was Vera Cruz. And when they got back to immigration, though four men were detained for questioning, Vera Cruz was not among them.

*

Excessive amounts of coffee didn't help anyone's frustration level as the assembled team laboriously crosschecked immigration cards against the passenger manifest. Jake had also requested the Pakistani authorities transmit the manifests of all flights departing from the same terminal within thirty minutes of the PIA aircraft. Had he requested help from another country, it might have been a straightforward affair. However, he hadn't factored in the inefficiencies of Pakistan's system, the language barrier, the time difference, and the large number of incorrectly documented passengers still awaiting clearance in UK immigration's holding lounge.

In the end, it was over four hours after the PIA flight landed before the team established Mario Bonetti had boarded the flight in Karachi, but hadn't disembarked in London, and a Peter Van der Vort had boarded a KLM flight from Karachi to Amsterdam, and had also landed at Heathrow.

As soon as he received the data entry findings, Jake was sure enough time had passed to enable his quarry to be long gone. Nevertheless, he posted an emergency alert to all European stations. Again, he'd been outwitted, and he hated that. It meant he'd forgotten to cover one of his bases. However, he had no doubt where final base was.

CHAPTER FORTY-TWO

Navigating Amsterdam's Schiphol airport is easy for a layman, so an experienced flyer knows that there are hourly departures to all UK airports. Locating the whereabouts of a Europa flight to Birmingham, Vera Cruz moved swiftly to the gate. Red was in the exact spot they had arranged to meet, but when she rushed forward, his mind was firmly concentrated on business. Gently pushing her away, he excused himself to the restroom.

It had become second nature for the captain to hide items in his flight bag, so as soon as he was out of surveillance camera range, he retrieved alternative passports for himself and Red in the names of John and Rachel McKinley. Then, donning sunglasses, he rejoined his "wife," handed her the passports and tickets, and took a seat to the side of the gate check-in counter.

Red completed the formalities, and at some point, the agent must have asked where John McKinley was. Their predetermined story was that her husband had chosen to sit away from the crowd as he was suffering from a migraine headache. When she called over and waved, Vera Cruz waved back. The gate agent was satisfied, and Mr. and Mrs. John McKinley received their business class boarding cards and were on their way to Birmingham International Airport.

CHAPTER FORTY-THREE

Jake's call had played havoc with Alex's mind, making manifest all the niggling doubts she had about her mysterious captain. However, in rewinding her mind video of the past couple of months, she was not willing to accept that Vera Cruz had used her. Yes, she had questions about him. But does anyone ever know everything about their partner? And yes, she had foolishly returned some passports to him, carried a picture to an unknown friend, and had driven across Europe in a car she knew was not his, to avoid paying duty. Did that really make her a criminal? And just because she and Jake had shared much, and he knew her so well, was it a sin that she didn't know diddly or talk about much of anything with Vera Cruz? Was it so bad that she and her lover were so physically compatible that she recalled little but the mind-blowing sex and that no matter what happened, they ended up in bed?

As Jake's assertion that she was desperate for love and obsessed with a womanizing con man reverberated in Alex's head, she smiled. She'd always been a realist, a woman who never automatically took the side of whoever shouted the loudest, and about now, it was Jake doing all the shouting. Well, he could shout all he wanted—she would figure out the facts for herself. And her first step would be to prove her lover's innocence. Resolve replaced Alex's tears.

After getting her car back, Alex had stowed Vera Cruz's flight bag in the under-stairs cupboard. Now, as she opened the door revealing the standard black leather case in its resting place, waves of guilt flooded over her. She was passionately opposed to invading another's privacy, and recalled how angry she'd been at Jake's intrusion into her life. But surely this was different. Her breathing increased to the point of hyperventilation. She had no choice. If for no other reason than to prove Jake wrong, she had to look inside the case.

After fetching kitchen scissors to sever the customs banding, Alex pulled the bag from its storage spot. Sitting beside it on the hall carpet, she took a deep breath and cut. Free of binding, she flipped the locks, but the combination held. Then, figuring she might just as well be hung for a sheep as a lamb, she carried the bag out to the garage, and popped the locks with a screwdriver and hammer.

The bag held more than she'd imagined, and being too cold outside to stand and review the contents, she lugged the bag back onto the kitchen table. Her initial riffling brought satisfied relief. She found flight manuals, assorted airline papers, and a toiletry bag. There was nothing to indicate the man she loved was anything other than a working pilot.

As her breathing calmed, Alex smiled. She'd wrecked Vera Cruz's bag, but when he'd wanted his passport, he told her to break the locks. She'd say it was done before he told her not to bother. A white lie was a small price to pay for the heaviness lifted from her heart. She was about to close the top when the floral patterned edges of some paper caught her attention. And though she had no grounds to question whether such decorative stationery was odd for a man to carry around, something deep inside her compelled her to take it out.

Experience might have taught her that curiosity often preceded bitter disappointment, nevertheless, Alex was obliged to read the pages.

She discovered a passionate love letter from a woman called Adele, and as she read on, part of her was ashamed to intrude on such very private thoughts. However, when the missive's bottom indicated more followed, for reasons inexplicable, she wanted to see more. She dug deep into the bottom of the bag, and found what she was looking for along with a number of other letters. They were in different hands, from women in several countries, and they all documented the writer's love and devotion. And while she'd long accepted Vera Cruz had had relationships before her, she was vaguely disturbed to note the letters were all recently dated.

She couldn't help smiling as their tone and content vividly reminded her why Vera Cruz was so accomplished in bed. But fascinated as she was with the uninhibited documentation of her lover's sexual habits, she wasn't sure she approved of his exceedingly casual attitude to multiple sex partners. Then she caught herself. How could she be so judgmental? Didn't he tell her more than once he had other women? And hadn't he admitted his expertise came from experience? Moreover, having participated wholeheartedly in his carnal circus, why did she imagine he'd be any less creative with other women? Who was she to complain now? Didn't she enjoy what he did to her?

But she was torn. Wasn't she special? Didn't she mean more? And then reality bit as Jake's words echoed. "I'm so sorry to be right about this." Her spirit hardened. Hardened because she realized, with actual proof of Vera Cruz's dalliances, she didn't like the situation any more than Jake did.

As she carefully refolded the letters, Alex couldn't prevent doubt from creeping in. Seriously, why would Vera Cruz be any more loyal to her than these other women? She decided it wouldn't be wise to pry any further. Jealousy and a certain amount of bitterness were coloring her attitude. When Vera Cruz arrived, she and he would talk through everything.

Alex dispersed the correspondence randomly in Vera Cruz's bag. It was more for her piece of mind than because he might recognize someone had rearranged his things. And she was delighted that apart from a bunch of torrid letters from multiple lady-friends, Jake had been wrong. She'd vindicated her lover. There was nothing remotely illegal in his bag. And as she formulated what she would say to her overly judgmental policeman friend, she pulled out a manual to hide the last letter. In doing so, she disturbed something between its pages.

For a second or two, Alex simply stared blankly at the fallen article. It was a PIA envelope, and although it didn't initially bother her, something disturbingly familiar registered. Then the cold light of recognition hit her squarely between the eyes. It wasn't that the stationery was the kind handed out in an airline's first-class cabin, or that it was unopened, or bore a Karachi postmark. It was the name—Captain Velasquez c/o PIA operations in Lisbon. Meaningless at the time she'd first heard it, the name now screamed at her to take notice. And as something dark and primeval rose within her, a frigid, empty dread hung over her.

Setting her jaw, anger overtook Alex. And without regard for Vera Cruz or anyone else's finer feelings, she tore open the envelope.

The writing, artistically rounded, carefully formed, almost childlike, was clearly the hand of a woman. And its neat curves and deliberately pressured ink were garishly interrupted by the occasional splotch, which she could only imagine were tears. Her heart went out to the writer who expressed her feelings for Vera Cruz in tender loving terms. But no one could ignore the underlying desperation of the words.

As an imperceptible shake started in Alex's fingertips, spread insidiously through chilled hands, and caused blood to pound in her temples, she felt something happening from which there would be no escape. She read on as the clearly defeated writer's words struggled across the page.

Expressing sorrow at being a disappointment to her lover, the writer tendered devotion to her family and their way of life. But she could go on no longer. Spent and broken, she was unable to live within a network of lies. The shame of what she'd done would haunt her and her family for the rest of their lives, and she couldn't stand the thought of a life in prison in Pakistan. But she was at peace with herself, resigned to making things right, and committed to her final decision. She ended the letter "yours forever and always," and her signature followed, lost and detached, alone in the corner.

"Maleka" burned into Alex's consciousness.

Dropping the letter like it was red-hot, a dozen incongruous pieces of Alex's life puzzle connected. She knew Maleka was the PIA flight attendant who'd committed suicide rather than face the consequences of smuggling drugs for Vera Cruz. But when the mysterious midnight caller had warned her of the pilot's mission, she had chosen to ignore him. A tear slid from her eye as she realized Maleka's letter was a damning testament to a soul destroyed, and showed the full measure of Vera Cruz's brutal reality.

And where was the "new" passport Vera Cruz said she would find? She'd been through every item, there was no passport. Then she recalled how many excuses had been made, how many lies had been left unchallenged, and how many times she'd looked the other way. She'd been blind and stupid, and just like all the rest, she'd been used. Everything Jake said about Vera Cruz was probably true, and her acceptance of the pilot's betrayal of all things good and decent hit her.

As Alex's shame and rage exploded, she swept the bag from the table. It hit the floor with a dull thud. Angrier with herself, Vera Cruz, and the bag than she ever imagined she could be, she kicked it with such possessed strength it rocketed across the room.

The brutalized bag settled against the wall, with everything she'd taken care to replace spilled out. Then her eyes locked on a pack of cigarettes and a lighter spinning conspicuously inappropriate on the tiled floor. Vera Cruz didn't smoke, though she didn't give a damn about the cigarettes. His vices were far more despicable. But the lighter proved an irresistible lure. Stepping over the bag, she picked it up. It was very feminine, like a piece of jewelry. Solid gold set across the bottom with several colored gems so tactile she couldn't help running her thumb over its intricately textured surface. And as she did so, a faint clicking sound directed her attention to the upended bag. It appeared her thumb pressure on the gems had released a secret compartment at the base of the bag, exposing an assortment of items packed in a preformed foam medium.

For several seconds Alex stared in stunned silence, unsure what she might do about the discovery. Then her curiosity piqued and, taking a long wooden spoon from a drawer, she poked the exposed compartment. Nothing happened. And after two hefty whacks elicited no movement, she reached inside the compartment, removing three passports and a large wad of American bills. Deeper probing revealed a velvet pouch containing what appeared to be diamonds, a gun made of some sort of polymer substance, and a small plastic sleeve. More curious than was good for anybody, but determined to get to the bottom of Vera Cruz's deception, she poured out the contents of the sleeve, her palm littered with tiny strips of film. And with Jake's words echoing loud in her head, Alex was no longer angry. She was very, very frightened.

CHAPTER FORTY-FOUR

The trio had spent but minutes at Red's house to exchange vehicles, check messages, and collect Pete's weapon. However, by the time they headed for Alex's house, snow was falling. It quickly became heavy, and as they hit the rural roads, the deeply rutted snow-pack slowed them down.

Vera Cruz wasn't particularly worried about a late arrival. Jim's message had said Alex was on a day off, and he knew that whatever time he appeared, she would welcome him in. But he was concerned the police were on to them. And while they'd seen no signs of an increased police presence along the route, he had Pete extinguish his lights as he turned onto Mulberry Lane.

It was a slow haul toward Alex's cottage as the lane was several miles long and unlit, but Vera Cruz forgot nothing. He remembered the farmhouse set back on the right and a lay-by to turn around farm vehicles just before a bend in the road. And there was a ditch in front of a hedge on either side of the lane from the farm all the way to Alex's cottage. He knew that if there were a police vehicle here, it would have to park conspicuously in the turn-around, or settle in a small gap in the hedge where a stile allowed hikers and hunters to get into the field. As they approached the stile, the bright moonlight threw a vague shadow across a beat-up van set right into the gap. Vera Cruz touched his associate's arm, and with an understanding nod Pete stopped and backed into the farm vehicle's turnaround.

As Pete got out of the car, Red took the controls and Vera Cruz remained in the seat beside her. They watched their associate climb over the turn-around snow bank, get behind the hedge, and trek through the snow toward the van. Then Red waited five minutes, and with Vera Cruz crouching in the passenger seat, she moved down the lane to pull up alongside the parked vehicle.

*

In the van's enveloping cocoon, the young police officer was totally unaware of what was taking place outside. He'd just called in a midnight check to dispatch and after replacing the radio handset, rolled down the window and lit a cigarette. As he took the first long drag, a Range Rover appeared from the darkness, pulled parallel, and he watched as the window rolled slowly down.

"Excuse me," the woman said. "I'm terribly lost; would you know the way to Warwick?"

Before he could answer, a man appeared from behind the hedge and fired one shot through the van's windshield.

With a quizzical look at the growing patch of scarlet on his chest, the stricken officer coughed, cigarette hanging motionless on his lip. Critically injured, he slumped to one side with his head half out of the open window. And as the cigarette dropped and sizzled dead on the snow-covered tarmac, the shooter came around the van, placed the tip of the silencer on the top of the policeman's head, and shot him again.

CHAPTER FORTY-FIVE

As Alex digested the disturbing facts lying all over her kitchen, she arrived at the only conclusion that made any sense. She must call Jake to come collect the bag. With shaking hands she hit redial and was connected to his home number. She complied with his machine and left a message. Next, she dialed his cell. It said "out of range." Counting to fifty, she tried again, static. Alex cursed. Where was his "call me anytime if you want to give me the bag" if she couldn't get hold of him? He'd worked over Christmas, so like her he was probably off duty until after the New Year. Was he simply so mad after their last exchange he wanted her to agonize? Or might he actually be somewhere he couldn't talk to her? In her heart she knew that was it. It didn't help.

Pulling herself into action mode, Alex recalled what Vera Cruz had said about picking up his bag around the New Year. She was determined to do whatever was necessary to avoid giving him the bag, and decided to return it to its hiding place. If he turned up before Jake, she'd tell him the police had it.

Alex hastily packed the manuals and papers back into the bag. However, when she tried to return the items to the concealed compartment, it appeared her assault had damaged the mechanism. The drawer wouldn't open far enough for her to replace the items in their foam indentations, and after several attempts at wiggling and hitting it with a rolling pin, it wouldn't close. She wedged everything in top of the bag and hauled the awkward bundle back under the stairs. Unfortunately, with the bag's broken compartment and over-stuffed top, the cupboard's junk, and the acute roof angle, she couldn't get in back in place.

As she wrestled the bag from the cubby, Alex recognized that had the situation not been so serious, she'd have found the whole cloak and dagger predicament funny. Instead, she silently berated herself for getting into such a mess and dumped out the ill-fitting items. Relieved of bulk at the top, she was able to finesse the bag into place. But now, she had to hide the compartment's contents in other places.

*

As she returned to the kitchen, with her mission accomplished, the phone rang. But should she answer it? What if it was Vera Cruz, on the way to pick up his bag? Could she remain calm now that she knew who he was and what he was doing? She could let the machine pick up. If he thought she wasn't there, it would give her time to re-call Jake. But Vera Cruz always seemed to know where she was, and for how long. Did he have people watching her? Were they watching her now? She froze as a thousand scenarios, one direr than the next, swamped her reason. Then the message machine kicked in.

"Alex, are you there? For God's sake, pick up."

She dived at the phone. "Jake, where are you? I've been trying to get you all evening, the phone kept telling me you were out of range."

"The snow caused a problem for a while, then I tried to call, your line was busy."

"Duh . . . calling you. Jesus, why is call waiting, and God alone knows what all else, only appropriate *after* some desperate jam makes you reali—"

"Alex, be quiet, that's not important now."

"Yes, it is. I really needed to get hold of you because everything you said about Vera Cruz is right. I found the film, and passports, and letters, and a gun. I am so stupid and I am so sorr—"

"Alex, calm down and listen to me. Get out now. He's coming for the bag. You cannot be there when he arrives."

"But I found the film. He can't have it—thousands of people might die."

"Right now my concern is for one person. We'll deal with the rest when you're safe."

"I can't just—"

"You can and you will. Put the frigging film in your pocket. Just leave, immediately. Go to the end of the street. There's a cop there, he's armed and he'll get you away. I've told the locals you need help and they'll get there as soon as they can and pick up Vera Cruz when he gets to the house. I'm getting in a helicopter right now."

"It's snowing, nobody can fly in this."

"Darling, please, for once, don't give me an argument. I'm coming to get you, now go. There's no time to—"

Just then there was a noise outside. "Jake, I heard a car. Somebody's here. What do I do?"

"Alex, listen to me carefully, you need to be thinking straight. It could be the local police. But if it's Vera Cruz, do whatever he wants, use up time. Give him the damn film if you have to."

"You know my history, and he's a terrorist! I'm not giving him any—"

"I'm begging you, darling. I can't lose another woman I love. Whatever it takes, find a way to use up ti—"

The phone made a hollow sound and she hit the receiver. There was no dial tone. She assumed the snow had brought down a line, and suddenly realized how vulnerable she was. Her mind instantly focused. She'd taped the film to the base of Jake's snow globe. She'd grab it and when Vera Cruz tapped on the front door, she'd sneak out the back and run to the cop along the street. She'd barely pulled on her boots when a feeling of foreboding overtook her.

Moving to the darkened living room's front window, she inched aside the curtains. She breathed a sigh of relief. There were two figures approaching the house. They must be the cops Jake sent. However, as she reached to switch on the lights, another apprehensive shiver swept over her. Something didn't feel right. Even local cops couldn't get here that fast. The snow was knee deep and she was in the middle of nowhere.

Peeping from behind the curtains again, Alex tried to make out who was coming to the door. However, before her eyes focused, the vestibule's automatic light popped on, near blinding her. When the spots from optic shock were gone, she saw Vera Cruz. The second figure was gone. With the hair on her arms bristling, Alex shuddered. Something odd was most definitely happening, and the urge to get out of the house was overwhelming.

The doorbell clanged louder than bells for Sunday service and, feeling a long-dormant instinct guiding her actions, Alex retreated to the kitchen. Counter lights sharply lit the area, so she kept low. Crouching beneath the phone, she reached up, yanked at the cord, and the handset fell noiselessly into her hands. She hit "talk" but there was nothing but empty air. The line was dead. *Now would have been a good time for that cell phone I swore I'd never buy.* Sitting back to the wall, she took several deep mind-clearing breaths, and crawled to the back door.

Her impatient visitor was done with doorbells and rapped on the door.

Calm and resolute, Alex quietly released the back door's bolt, and Jake popped into her head, screaming, "Get in the car!" Then she saw another shadow behind the kitchen blinds. It must be the other person she saw approaching the house. *Breathe, breathe,* she told herself, and dropped to the floor. *Escape,* her mind screamed, *in the car, now.* Crawling and clawing, she flipped her car keys off the hook and returned to the garage. But the car's auto lock had engaged and she couldn't insert the key. The lock was frozen. As she stepped back to the kitchen and pulled de-icer from the closet, she heard a window break. Someone was breaking into the garage. *Shit . . . shit. Lock the door.* She barely slid the bolt when she heard rustling.

Eyes wide, blood pounding in her temples, Alex watched the knob slowly turn. Then a resounding thud hit the door, but it held. Scooting back, she slumped against the counter, head aching from the pressure of gritted teeth. *Don't be afraid, you can do this. Breathe . . . breathe. What to do? Think! Policeman at the end of the lane; will be there no matter what. Bless you, dearest Jake. Can't get out the back way, so let Vera Cruz in, get outside, scream like a banshee and run like hell. Okay . . . breathe . . . breathe . . . you can do this.*

The rapping at the front door had become a pounding. But now her mind was sharp with the chemicals of self-preservation. She forced the pain of recent revelations aside and took a calming breath. As she approached the front door, Vera Cruz called out her name.

"Alex, it's me, open the door."

His voice was exactly as she remembered it, and she opened the door a crack. However, while she remembered his voice exactly, the discoveries of the last hour had tarnished her memory of his face. As she looked at him, she had forgotten how handsome he was, how disarming and frighteningly hypnotic.

She widened the door's gap and, craving reassurance, looked into his eyes. Someone she didn't know stared back. And what she now saw behind his eyes frightened her.

*

"Tayo, it's you. I wasn't expecting—"

"What kept you?" He looked at her and his voice hardened. "I saw the curtains move. Didn't you see me?" Brushing by her, he entered the darkness of the living room.

"Sleep, I was asleep. Thought I was dreaming, then I heard you call my name."

Vera Cruz noticed lights on in the kitchen, and that she had boots on. "I didn't call your name until just now." He pulled her into his embrace and she shrunk from him.

"Really? I must have been dreaming then. About you . . . er . . . us . . . and the wonderful times we've had."

Looking at her face, he wondered whether she was trying to play him for a fool. It wasn't sleep making her distant. She knew. Knew who he was, and what he did with his life. And most importantly, she knew exactly what he'd come for. "Umm . . . wonderful? Is that how you see our time together?"

He didn't bother putting on the fake accent Alex was used to hearing, and she realized she didn't know him at all. "Of course, don't you?"

Vera Cruz kissed his finger and tapped her nose. And as he turned to switch on a lamp beside the sofa, Alex moved. She got as far as the front door when *smack*! Red stepped from the shadows, blocking her exit. Smiling sadistically, she pushed Alex hard back into the living room. Alex staggered but regained her footing and tried to dodge by her assailant. Red stood her ground and, knowing she had the upper hand, shut the door behind her.

"You know," said Vera Cruz, grabbing Alex's arm and pulling her close. "You have to work on your body language. It'll give you away every time."

She tried to pull away. "Tayo, stop, you're hurting my arm."

He held fast. "Now what sort of a greeting is this? Don't I get a kiss?"

He savagely crushed his mouth on hers, but Alex squirmed violently and pushed him away.

Red sidled by them into the kitchen. "Looks like you lost this one, captain." She chuckled.

The laugh irritated Vera Cruz. "Now that," he said, shaking Alex violently, "is just plain rude. I'm going to have to teach you some manners." He pushed her hard onto the couch.

*

As Alex gained her composure, she felt a presence behind her and turned. Close up she could see it was the redhead who'd collected the picture at Heathrow. Now she was casually sipping a glass of wine, while her other hand held up Jake's business card.

Vera Cruz snatched it. "Who the hell have you been talking to?" Before Alex could answer, he had her by the hair and pulled her to her feet. "Go get my bag."

"Can't." Alex winced. "Police took it."

"When?" He tightened his grip on her hair.

"Yesterday. Came here to ask about it. Said it was given to me by mistake, so I gave it back to them."

"You're not a very good liar, my dear."

"It's the truth. Jake is a friend, he said he'd deal with it."

Vera Cruz held Jake's card inches from her face. "Why would Special Branch be interested in a lost crew bag? Even if it was given to you by mistake, it's a customs issue. Being staff, they would merely tell you to return it when you went into work. IT WOULD BE NO BIG DEAL." His face, wrath spitting close to hers, radiated evil. "Unless, of course, they, and now you, know what's inside it." His voice rasped menacing in her ear. "You know what's inside, don't you?"

"Don't know anything. Didn't open it, just gave it back to the police. Why are you doing this to me?"

"Because I can, and what's more, you will really learn what I can do to you if you don't tell me where the fuck my bag is."

"I told you, I don't know anything about your bag or what's in it. They asked for it, I gave it to them."

"Then why, Miss Mack, are you so frightened of me? From the minute you opened the door there's been a look of terror on your face." He dug his fingers deeper into her cheeks. "Remember, I have done things to you no other man has done. I have enjoyed every inch of your body and felt every emotion you possess. But this . . . " He shook her head. "This is new. This face is angry. These eyes show defiance, and *that* I have never felt."

"It's not what you think. You're scaring me. Please let me go, I don't know anything."

"Well, I don't think my little passenger handler is being entirely honest. You see I'm really good at this. I can read things, especially in stupid spoiled bitches like you. And here . . . " He swirled his fingers close to her face. "Here we have disgust."

"No, I'm shocked is all, let me go now, I won't say anything to anyone. No one will ever know you were here."

"Why should you think I care if anyone knows I'm here?" He shook her again. "I'll tell you why. Because you know who I am, and what's in my bag."

Alex attempted to wriggle from his grasp, but only succeeded in angering him further.

"Stop that now, or I will hurt you. Information might be power, my dear, but in your case, as I'm sure your policeman friend told you, it will merely serve to exacerbate the damage I might do to you." Bending her head, he bit vampire-like into her neck. "Come see this, Red," he said to his companion. "Something new to think about." He'd left a developing corona of bruising around the clearly defined marks left by his teeth. "Do you think I could bite hard enough to have her bleed out?"

Alex fought the urge to scream, and flailed impotently.

"Won't know unless you try," said Red, running her finger over the welt.

Vera Cruz smiled. "Search the place, we're going to bed."

Alex fought for footing as Vera Cruz dragged her upstairs. She swatted and struggled, but he didn't let her go until they were in the bedroom.

"Alex, stop," he whispered. "I am so sorry for all that downstairs. I know you probably hate me about now, but I'm in deep trouble with these people and I have to make them think I'll hurt you."

"And you won't?"

"Of course not. But they are ruthless and if they thought for one second I was being soft on you, we'd both be dead."

"All that shoving and pushing was an act?"

Pulling her into his arms, he kissed her tenderly. "What do you think? You have to believe me, I am so sorry. Everything will be okay if you simply give her the bag."

"I told you, it's not here."

"Alex, please. We have had wonderful times together, you know in your heart I wouldn't lie to you."

"Like you didn't lie to the others?" She bit her lip as soon as she said it. "I'm sorry. I did look in the bag. I found a bunch of love letters."

"I told you there were others. You aren't the same as those women. They meant nothing to me."

"What about her downstairs? Wasn't she the one who picked up the picture?"

"She's a courier, that's what she does. Give her the bag and she'll leave. Then we can go back to where we left off." He un-cinched her robe and ran his fingers over her breasts. "You know how good we are together, and how special you are to me."

Jake's words flooded Alex's mind: "Do whatever he wants, use up time."

With her heart thumping, hostility forcing adrenaline into her system, Alex peeled off her nightgown. "How special?"

Vera Cruz simply stared at her naked vulnerability and smiled. It was several seconds before he moved. And when he did, it was to run his knuckles gently down her cheek, along her shoulders, and across her breasts. "So it seems I'm forgiven. Do you want me to make love to you?"

Trembling with fury, Alex couldn't prevent tears welling. "Yes."

Vera Cruz continued to run his hands over her body. "Relax.

Let me make you feel good." He encountered charged nipples, and took one into his mouth.

She couldn't stop her body reacting, and when his fingers gently explored inside her, a moan purred deep in her throat.

He gently laid her on the bed and, having shucked his clothes, lay alongside her. "You read all the letters?" he asked.

"No," she lied. "They were too personal."

"Well, thank you for that." He pecked her on the lips. "What else did you find?"

"Nothing. Now make love to me."

He moved atop her and slid easily inside. "This feels good, you really did miss me, didn't you?"

"Yes, now stop talking and work." Alex relaxed as he moved slowly and deliberately, but resolve quickly took over and she matched his rhythm and dragged him deep. "You're going to have to do a lot better than that." She bit into his shoulder, and his speed and depth increased. But as she looked up at him, the bright light of desire she'd once read in his eyes was replaced by something cold, calculating, and deadly. It didn't matter, it was her time now. She was in control. She was the one with contempt in her heart. And she would make him pay.

Alex moaned softly. It was easy to lie, and as she glanced at their reflection in the closet mirror, she could hardly believe what she was doing. Hardly believe it, but doing it anyway. And as she matched him stroke for stroke, rotating her hips and pulling him in, she repeated to herself, *use up time, use up time.*

And then Vera Cruz stopped.

"No, no, no," she complained. "Keep going."

He leaned down, sucked on a nipple, and kissed her lightly on the mouth. "Something's not right here."

"It's perfect, come on, I want you inside me."

"No, you don't. Alex, it's me. I know every inch of your body. And I know for sure that the last thing you want is me inside you."

He propped himself on one elbow. "There's no escape, you know that. Now let's enjoy each other one last time, you give me my bag, and we'll get out of here."

She spat in his face. "Fuck you."

He swiped at the spittle. "Such language from a lady. I had no idea you had it in you."

"Go to hell."

Vera Cruz put a hand around her throat and began to cut off her oxygen.

She flailed at him until she became light-headed. All she cared about was protecting the stuff from his bag. Whether she lived or died, he wasn't getting it. She gasped for air until everything went black.

*

Vera Cruz knew the exact second when Alex's unconsciousness occurred. He'd played the choking sex game with Red many times and the high it gave them was unmatched. As Alex fell limp, her lips tinged blue, he released his hands and shook her to life. His face was very close to hers as she gasped for air. "Now you're playing my sort of game. Feels good doesn't it, being so close to death and popping right back?"

"Death is preferable to being with you."

He smiled. "Now you really don't mean that." He ran his fingers down her belly and watched her nipples react. "See, your mind says one thing, your body the other. A little oxygen deprivation will soon have your mind exactly where I want it." His hand resumed its position on her neck.

"You can't make me do anything."

"Really?" His grip tightened. "You know I can keep up these little games all night. Now, last chance—where's my goddamn bag?"

"Told you, I gave it to the police, I don't know anything."

"You're lying—I can see it in your eyes. Don't play the innocent, you're in too deep."

"I've done nothing."

"Nothing? Well, let's review events. Wasn't it you who found, and failed to turn in, a bunch of forged passports? And didn't you carry a stolen painting, worth millions through customs? Weren't you with me when I drove a drug-loaded Alpha Romeo Spider into the UK? And, correct me if I'm wrong, but didn't you clear a flight bag that holds a special little something like, oh yeah, a terrorist's microfilm?"

"I didn't know, I trusted y—"

"Ignorance is no excuse and your dumb-ass trust doesn't matter. If I get caught, you'll spend as much time in prison as I do."

Tears of frustration and self-loathing fell down Alex's face, and a scream froze in her throat as Red appeared over Vera Cruz's shoulder.

"Look what I found, dearest," said Red, holding aloft the flight bag, secret compartment open and empty. "Seems your little pink mouse is a big fat liar."

Alex knew Vera Cruz would now fully vent his anger on her, and as she struggled to get from under him, he viciously punched her in the face. Tasting the warm, metallic, saltiness of blood, Alex summoned strength she didn't know she possessed and fought back. She got a hand free and fisted Vera Cruz in the mouth.

"Oh my," said Red, laughing. "Mouse has balls."

"Shut up," snapped Vera Cruz. "Watch and learn or get the hell out." Swiping a hand across his mouth and easing himself to his knees, he punched Alex full force in the abdomen.

She lay motionless as excruciating pain surged through her belly. She knew that there was no saving her now and as she lay winded, he fell on top of her and forced her legs apart. But Alex fought back. Clouting him several times, she saw that he enjoyed her violent response. She went limp, like a rag doll. And the tactic worked. "You can't hurt me anymore. I know who you are and what you're doing."

He punched her in the face again. "Shut up and let me think."

As Alex lay dazed, excruciating pain, red-hot and searing deep within, coursed through her abdomen. All she could do was focus on what Jake had said. As she pulled herself to the farthest corner of the bed, a third person appeared in the doorway. Alex recognized him as the driver in Rome.

"Boss," said Pete, focusing on Alex's nakedness. "No other cops in the area. Can I join the party?" He reached for his zipper.

"Now that's an idea. She's all warmed up so you can have a crack at her after you get rid of the car and the body."

Alex was horrified. Not at the news that Pete would be next with her, but that the policeman who'd been watching her was dead.

Seeing the look on her face, Vera Cruz laughed. "Oh look, poor little Alex realizes her knight in shining armor isn't coming to rescue her. And why? Because he's just a tiny bit dead. Get going, Pete. She'll keep 'til you get back."

Eager to complete the mission and claim his spoils, Pete re-zipped his jeans and left.

Devoid of emotion, Alex knew she'd brought this misery upon herself, and she stared blankly into space.

"You know, my dear," Vera Cruz said, reaching over to trace a finger through the trickle of blood running down her thigh. "You should be honored Pete gets to work on your soft, prissy body. He's an elephant of a man, and so creative in getting the best out of my property." He touched Alex's face, her broken nose, and split lip. Then he grabbed her hair and twisted her head back. "So where are the contents of my bag? And if you say 'I don't know,' believe me, I will have Pete make you wish you'd never been born."

"Bank, safety deposit box," Alex whispered.

"Now that sounds like the boring little mouse I know. So it seems you'll have the pleasure of our company for a few more hours."

"Screw you all."

"Oh my dear, such anger. You think I was hard on you? I'm a pussycat. Wait 'til you feel what Pete has in store. It'll be an education watching him work on you. Now clean yourself up, you're a mess."

Alex didn't care how she looked, but she wanted to get away. Sliding painfully from the bed, she staggered to the bathroom. But before she could close the door and block out the evil she was amid, she saw Red on her hands and knees on the edge of the bed with Vera Cruz hammering into her from behind.

*

With a bathroom full of mirrors, Alex got the first good look at herself. Her eyes were swollen shut, blood dribbled from her nose and lips, and bite marks on her breasts and neck glowed angry purple and blue. All of it was a pale reproduction of the pain she felt. And as she reached to turn on the shower, blood seeped down her legs and her abdomen throbbed. She knew Vera Cruz's punch had done some damage to her insides, and there was no way she could run anywhere. In her present condition, she wouldn't make it to the front door. Neither would she endure a sexual assault by Vera Cruz's accomplice. Those seconds of abject wretchedness told her what she must do.

Mind-numbing pain surged as Alex crouched down. Fighting the inclination to faint, she reached into the back of the sink's cabinet. She felt around for the gift basket Vera Cruz had given her for Christmas, gritted her teeth, and dragged it out. Then wrestling it onto the vanity, she spilled the bottles and jars into the sink, until only a piece of velvet material over a thick layer of padding remained. Rummaging beneath, Alex pulled out Vera Cruz's gun.

Feeling the delicate weight of the small plastic weapon, Alex was aware she knew nothing about guns. But she'd seen enough cop shows to know there was a safety catch somewhere and she'd have to release it. She wasn't even sure it was loaded, but knowing Vera Cruz as she now did, chances were good it was. Standing motionless, feeling the empowering warmth of the gun's handgrip, she knew there was only one way out for her now. All she could think about was whether or not she had the strength to hang on until Jake got there.

It took a few seconds for Alex to breathe deeply enough to gain composure. No one was going to inflict any more pain on her. And ignoring any consequences that might befall her, she straightened up as best she could, and stepped out of the bathroom.

With arms extended and hands wrapped together to calm the shaking, she repeated to herself, *you can do this, you can do this*. And as she rounded the corner into the bedroom, a shaft of moonlight fell on a photograph on the dresser.

It was a picture of her husband, happy and smiling, the Statue of Liberty over his shoulder. He'd e-mailed it to her the day he'd arrived in New York. It was the last she saw of him. He'd been in the first of the Twin Towers as it disintegrated on September 11, 2001. She so vividly remembered that day—how desolate she felt watching the tragedy unfold on television, how her life collapsed as completely as one floor melted down on another.

Then Jake's kind face flooded her mind. Jake, whose comforting words had changed everything. Jake, who had always been there and would never let her down. Jake, who was on the way to save her, because he loved her like no man ever had.

And her resolve solidified.

Now she didn't care that her actions might be perceived as equally criminal as the actions of the people before her. She simply knew no matter what personal price she had to pay, she wasn't going to let something like the Twin Towers happen again.

Alex moved quietly into the bedroom to find Red bouncing atop Vera Cruz, her eyes closed in lust-filled concentration. But when she detected Alex's presence, she opened them. Recognizing what was in Alex's outstretched hands she gasped, and frantically backed away from her partner.

Shocked at Red's abrupt departure, Vera Cruz sat up and followed the panic in her eyes. "Alex, don't be crazy," he said, voice as smooth as it had ever been. "You know you won't shoot, you don't have it in you." He sounded again like the Vera Cruz she had loved, but viciousness and contempt radiated from his eyes. Then his ego took over. "Look at you, standing there all naked and damaged. You're a pawn, a patsy, a silly little girl, you don't have the guts."

As he positioned himself to lunge, Alex cocked the weapon. It stopped him in his tracks, and Alex could see a chink in the confidence of his supercilious grin.

"You're wasting your time," he said. "It's not loaded."

As he sprang toward her, she fired three times. "That's for all the people you destroyed." Turning her gun on Red, she fired again. "And that one's for me."

Slumping to the floor, Alex held fast to the gun in case Pete returned. But before the reverberation of the gunshots quieted, she heard a helicopter overhead.

CHAPTER FORTY-SIX

"Alex," Jake whispered. "I'm here now. Let go of the gun."

"I killed them, Jake . . . my God . . . what have I done?"

"You didn't, darling. Come on, loosen your fingers, give me the gun."

As she looked up into his eyes, she saw unconditional love. How could she have missed that all these years? How could she not have known how he felt? And why would she ever have thought another man could give her what he offered? "You came for me."

"I told you I would. Here I have your robe."

"I couldn't let them—"

"I know, darling. It's okay. They'll live and so will you, but you need to get checked at the hospital."

"Can't . . . snow is downing the line and the moving is nowhere coming."

"It's stopped now. Darling, you're making no sense. You're in shock, so help me out here and put your arm in the sleeve."

"Hurts . . . " Alex pointed to her belly.

"I know. Okay, deep breath, I'm going to pick you up now."

The last thing she remembered as the world turned to black were his strong arms lifting her from the floor. Then she woke in the ambulance and he was there. And in the emergency room, it was Jake holding her hand, telling her everything would be all right.

*

The sun streamed through the window of the bedroom, and as she glanced around she realized she was in her parents' house. The radio alarm said it was just after noon and there on top, front and center, was her *Keystone Cops* snow-globe.

Jake came into the room and sat beside her. "Hey, sleepy, I've got soup."

"Have you been with me all the time?"

"I said I'd be there if you needed me. I think this qualifies."

"What about work?"

"I quit."

"You did not."

He smiled. "I had a bunch of vacation time coming. This seemed as good a place as any to hang out, and your mom's a fabulous cook."

"You're living here?"

"Yep. We finally get to sleep under the same roof. So are you going to sit up, or do I need to get a straw?"

"Fool."

"That's why you love me."

"How do you figure that?"

"You told me. Scoot up, I'll put some pillows behind you. No pain, right?"

"I'm good. When did I tell you I loved you?"

"In the ambulance."

"That doesn't count, I was in shock."

"You're taking it back?"

She never again wanted to be without his normalcy and quiet strength. "Not if you kiss me."

*

Eddie Barstow tugged at his collar. He never liked monkey suits. Jake, on the other hand, looked like he'd stepped from the pages of *GQ*. He turned as a frothy cloud of bridesmaids floated down the aisle of the small country church. He tugged Jake's sleeve.

"Hey man, is corraling all these nephews and nieces part of the best man's job?"

"Maid of honor."

"Thank God. There's a million of 'em."

"Yeah, it's cool, right?"

"If you say so." Eddie looked at his watch. "Do you think she's here yet?"

"Nope."

"And you're not nervous?"

"Been there, done that. She'll make it."

"That's pretty casual coming from you."

Jake smiled as Alex's words echoed: "Make it? I always make it. Maybe a little late sometimes, but I always get here."

As the organ struck up the wedding march, Jake turned. Alex was always the most beautiful woman he'd seen. Now she would be the most beautiful wife.

About the Author

Born and raised in Warwickshire, England, Anji began her adult life in the Women's Royal Air Force, and left the service to join British Airways at London's Heathrow Airport.

Immigrating to the United States in 1986, Anji worked in the human resources field writing manuals, training courses, and the like, ran a one-hundred-and-forty apartment senior community and during her last employment as Marketing Director for an adult care service, wrote a monthly column on Alzheimer's issues. She has lent her voice to local radio commercials, and participated in the veterans' video project held in the Library of Congress.

Anji is a world traveler who now resides in Northern Arizona. She has written five novels, *Desperate Obsession*, *Everything Comes If...*, *Lonely Hearts Cry*, *The Cormorant Club*, and *How Many Freakin' Frogs Do You Have To Kiss?* She is a member of the Mystery Writers of America, Romance Writers of America, the RWA-Women's Fiction, NARWA, RWA-Kiss of Death, and the Chick-lit Writers of the World.

In the mood for more Crimson Romance? Check out *The Achilles Project* by Jessica Starre at *CrimsonRomance.com*.